D0734766

# DEAD CENTER

**By the same author**
Dead Ahead

*To Joel and Sharon, Joan,*
*Miriam and Mark (in memoriam),*
*Ira and Becky, Jeffrey and Naomi*

*I am deeply indebted to my generous friend Bob, a retired NYPD detective. My fingers itch to add his last name, but he insists on remaining anonymous. On the force for over twenty-nine years, twenty-one of them in the Detective Bureau, he is a storehouse of knowledge, always willing to answer the pickiest question and share his expertise.*

*My gratitude also to Effie Manolas, who helped with the Greek words, their spelling and meaning.*

*And always, special thanks to my husband, Joe, who contributed in dozens of ways, including driving me through various parts of Brooklyn, New York so I could find a good place to leave a body.*

# 1

It wasn't just another case—Nikki thought she recognized the corpse, but with all the blood on his face she wasn't sure. He sat on the front seat of the big black Mercedes, head resting against the passenger window. Bright morning light showed the hole where the bullet had entered, at almost the exact center of his forehead. He was restful in death. Except for his painted face he might have been napping in this quiet parking lot near the water's edge in Brooklyn. Small craft bobbed in the marina below, gulls squealed overhead.

She checked his license plate and knew then she'd been right. "ZAP—1." Dean Zaporelli, city councilman. She'd seen him on talk shows, seen his picture in the paper. Why did so many good guys die young, while real bastards lived into their nineties? Zaporelli had fought to keep a shelter for the homeless open during the budget crunch last year, had donated some of his own money to fund it, had spent a night there to dramatize the need for support.

Trencher, the rookie who'd been first officer on the scene, hadn't identified Zaporelli when he'd called in. Nikki phoned the news into the station house, and word spread through the department like fire creeping through dry brush. Only 0930 hours on this late March morning, yet every big shot in Brooklyn felt he had to put in an appearance. Dritzer, the Borough Chief of Detectives. And of course, *his* boss, the

Chief of Detectives. The cops at the crime scene were supposed to bar the public; Nikki felt like telling them to keep the brass out too. Dritzer left a clear print of his right hand on top of the car when he leaned inside for a look. Detective Nikki Trakos knew by now how to tell an ordinary officer to get the hell out of the crime scene—how did she give the word to the chief? She'd have to make sure the latent print guys knew the print belonged to a friendly hand so they wouldn't spend hours looking for a match.

One by one the brass left, climbed into their cars and sped away. Her squad commander, J.J. Parcowicz, known familiarly as Eagle-Eye, was the last to go. He fixed her with his nearsighted stare. "It's *yours*, Trakos. Got that?"

"I got it."

And then the never-ending lecture: "Police work is teamwork, Trakos." Someday she would needlepoint that little bit, frame it, and hang it on his wall next to the sign that said, I'M NEVER WRONG—I'M THE BOSS. "I want to know where you are, what you're doing, every minute of the day," he said.

She was tempted to ask if she had to report her visits to the ladies' room but thought better of it. He liked her clearance record, her ability to pull a complicated case together. But it drove him wild that she went off on her own, found her solutions in a complicated process he had trouble following.

"Get those reports in, Trakos. Hear me?"

"I hear you."

She watched him pull away, thinking of the challenge of the case. She'd worked on five "little" murders in Brooklyn in the past year, closed each one. She'd hoped Eagle-Eye would put her name on the promotion list, but so far he hadn't. She suspected it was because she was a woman. Also, she'd been with the Detective Bureau only a year. But if she found Zaporelli's killer, got credit as case detective, he'd *have* to do something for her, wouldn't he?

Besides Zaporelli's car the parking lot was empty, an

oblong enclosed by a cyclone fence. It had once been used by a yacht club. The small weather-beaten office building was still standing. Right under the words SLIPS AVAILABLE, someone had stuck a sign saying CLOSED FOR REPAIRS. Nikki glanced down into the marina. The walkways looked rotted, unsafe. Out toward Jamaica Bay a big white party boat rode at anchor. It reminded her of the one her father had owned, the *Poseidon*. As a teen-ager, Nikki had worked as his mate, cutting bait, filleting fish, swabbing decks.

The neighborhood was residential, rows of one- and two-family houses side by side. Small garden strips fronted each house. The gardens were still winter-hard though it had officially become spring last week. Eagle-Eye had divided the area, assigned teams to question residents on Bijou Avenue and poke through nearby trash cans. He'd ordered an auto canvass—license plate numbers on Bijou all the way down to Gerritsen and on some of the nearby side streets. The numbers would be run through the computer for any useful information they might yield.

A nagging worry chewed at Nikki as she watched the crime-scene technicians work. She'd done everything the case detective was supposed to do, but she felt as though she were forgetting something. She seemed to be operating with half a brain this morning. She kept missing Dave Lawton, the homicide squad detective who'd partnered her on previous murders. They'd worked well as a team, pitching ideas back and forth, brainstorming together, giving each other leads. She had to stop thinking about him, couldn't allow herself to become distracted.

She backed off some feet from the car to where Joe Stavich stood. Stavich, her new partner from the homicide squad, was barrel chested, wore a crew cut, had a nose curved like a parrot's beak. He was average height, five eight or nine, inches shorter than Nikki's six feet.

When they'd met this morning the first thing he'd said

was, "I got a daughter your age." What was he saying? That at thirty-one she was too young to handle the case? She'd worn her "power outfit," a black-and-white checked jacket, trim black skirt, tailored blouse. Her brown hair was less than shoulder length, shining and neat. It was a no-nonsense, all-professional look, yet Stavich didn't seem to buy it.

Meekins, the blond crime-scene tech, and his partner lifted cameras out of their van. Nikki said, "Give me as much as you can on the car. The outside, the interior. Every angle."

"You got it," Meekins said.

When they were through she bent into the Mercedes for another look, leaned in from the driver's side, stooping down, careful not to touch anything. She turned to Stavich. "Can I show you something?"

He took a step in her direction. Was it his small eyes, hidden behind folds of flesh, that made him look bored? Or had he been on the job too long, seen too much? She wondered if she'd done the right thing asking not to have Dave on this case. She'd had to head him off—it was a clear instance of her personal life interfering with her professional life. But now she felt overwhelmed by the size of this case, weighed down by responsibility. She wasn't comfortable with Stavich, wondered if it was just that she wasn't used to him. A damp breeze lifting off Jamaica Bay seemed to penetrate to her skin, adding to the uneasiness she felt. The wind had picked up. The boats in the marina tossed against one another like toys in a bathtub.

She pointed toward the seat of the Mercedes. Dull brown trails marked the upholstery, starting on the driver's side and ending on the passenger's, under the body. "See the way the blood goes?" she said to Stavich. "Runs that way. There's less where he's sitting."

"So?"

"He got it while he was behind the wheel, and the shooter moved him."

Stavich made a face. "Nah, I don't see it that way." He shook a Camel out of a pack, lit it with a plastic lighter. He was the classic chain-smoker, his stubby fingers yellowed by nicotine. "If he got it while he was driving, how come the car didn't go out of control?"

"They were stopped for something," she said. "A light, or a stop sign. Or they were parked." The keys were still in the ignition, swinging on a chain. "Maybe somewhere nearby. The perp shoots him, then drives the car over here."

"That's one theory," Stavich said, as though it couldn't possibly hold water. He shifted his glance across the parking lot toward the crowd of uniforms at the ribbon. Nikki got the feeling the discussion was closed.

The hell with him. She tried to imagine how Dave would handle the case if he were here, what questions he would ask. She pictured his quick, dark eyes, the cherublike look hiding the intelligence and toughness. Thinking about Dave upset her. She'd done what she had to do, asking for another partner, but the more she thought about it the less sure she was Dave would understand why. But, it was done, over with. He had to accept it. She turned back to the body.

The challenge of the case charged her with excitement. She didn't see the still, silent corpse but the man as he had been just before his death. She felt his shock as the gun appeared, his terror when he realized he was about to die. And even though it was only Day One, early on, she'd begun to think about the other figure—the one who held the gun. He or she was still unseen, layered in mystery. What had the two been talking about before the fatal shot? Had they fought? And afterward, how had the killer made his escape?

Zaporelli was handsome—or had been. Late thirties or early forties, thick dark hair over a high forehead, large slanted eyes. She remembered watching him campaign on TV, thinking he would get the women's vote for sure. He'd fought for "women's" issues, too. Besides his special interest in the homeless, he'd supported city-run day-care centers, after-school care for ghetto kids. She felt another twist of anger that his voice had been silenced, his work cut short.

How had he ended up in a parking lot way out near the Brooklyn shore? He belonged to Manhattan, the *real* Big Apple. Brooklyn was only its stem. He'd been found here at six this morning, by a woman walking her dog. Case No. 416 for the current year.

Meekins, the blond tech, unwrapped a fresh stick of gum. "I wasn't gonna vote for him anyhow," he said to Nikki. "He didn't have to kill himself."

"You should've told him that," Nikki said.

She was determined not to let her anxiety show. Her first high-profile case. There would be a cast of thousands, detectives in all five boroughs looking to make a name for themselves, descending on the precinct. But in the end the responsibility would be hers, the case detective's.

She glanced across the lot. A CBS news truck had pulled up on Bijou. Cameramen unloaded equipment from the rear. Another spike of uneasiness jabbed at her—how would she be when her name was in all the newspapers, when the Borough Chief and Chief of Detectives trailed her around, pressed her for results? And what about Eagle-Eye? When the pressure was on, he'd want to keep constant tabs on her.

She shoved her cold hands into the pockets of her suit jacket, telling herself she would be okay.

Meekins laid a plastic sheet on the ground. "He was gonna announce for the Assembly next week," he said. Light vapor rose from his mouth as he spoke.

"He ain't announcing nothing now," his partner, the dark-haired tech, said. Nikki had met the two of them a year ago on her first homicide, the Sunmann case, and since then had worked with them on five more. She could never remember the dark-haired tech's name.

Behind the ribbon two more police cars pulled up. Bijou was crowded with blue-and-whites now, the street gay as a maypole. Mitchell, the patrol sergeant, climbed out of the first car. Two more uniforms emerged from the second, joining the knot of cops holding back the growing crowd. An NBC van had parked behind the CBS vehicle. A reporter with a hand-held mike interviewed a woman.

Meekins glanced toward Stavich. "I see Davy ain't working this one with you," he said to Nikki.

Her face grew warm. "He couldn't make it," she lied. She'd left Dave's house last night feeling as though their relationship were racing ahead at too frightening a clip, as though she were on a runaway sled and couldn't jump off. This morning when she'd caught the case she'd said to Eagle-Eye, "I want someone besides Lawton—need a change." She'd asked him not to mention her request to Dave.

The two techs lifted Zaporelli from the car, laid him down on a plastic sheet. Mitchell, the white-haired patrol sergeant, ducked under the ribbon and started toward her with Trencher at his side. At a certain angle Mitchell was a dead ringer for her Uncle Spyros, the cop. That, and his encouragement of her, always made Nikki glad to see him. He took her off to the side, asked gently, "How're you doing?"

She flip-flopped her hand.

"Because it's a headliner?"

"Yes."

"You'll do fine." His eyes were the same rich brown as her uncle's had been, the same color as Nikki's mother's and father's, most of her family. Nikki was among the handful who had blue eyes. Her grandmother had explained to her how this had come about. "God looked down after He created you, and he wanted to do something extra special for you. He looked in his *servan*, his cabinet, and he found this paint he'd been saving from when he made the Aegean."

Meekins asked Nikki, "Want anything else on the car before it gets towed?" The Mercedes would be taken to the station house, dusted for prints, and searched.

"Give the trunk and glove compartment a quick look."

The trunk was empty. The dark-haired tech turned the key in the glove compartment, reached inside, pulled out a manila envelope. He opened it and straightened suddenly. "Perp left you a present."

It was a .38 caliber Colt revolver, its cylinder gleaming blue in the morning light.

Stavich said, "Hey, what a break! Maybe the perp put his name and address on it, too."

"No slugs to make a match," Nikki said. "They're probably in Zaporelli or the car."

"Nah," Stavich said. "There ain't any holes in the car. Nothin' you can see from a quick look. Anyhow, most slugs are so mashed you can't read 'em. I bet ya my pension, right now, that ain't the gun."

The tech held the Colt by its grip, used a small feathered brush to flick on the white dusting powder. Nikki and the others stood where they were, watching. The tech shook his head. "Only a coupla smudges."

"I'm tellin ya," Stavich said, "that ain't the gun."

"Looks like Zaporelli got it in one hit," Nikki said. "So if we don't find the slug or it's unreadable, there's no way we can say whether it is or not."

The dark-haired tech put the Colt into a plastic evidence bag. "I *bet* it is," he said. "We didn't see no casings." Unlike an automatic, a revolver retained its fired cartridge cases.

Mitchell ducked his head inside the Mercedes. "The car's clean."

"Too clean," Nikki said. "No slugs, no shells, no holes. No broken glass." She glanced at Mitchell. "A professional?"

He shook his head. "Not with one hit, Nikki. Those guys earn their fee." Mitchell was the only cop at the precinct who called her Nikki instead of Trakos. When he did that he reminded her even more of her mother's brother Spyros, the cop who'd been her childhood hero. She missed Spyros, who'd died three years ago. For a moment she was a child again, an over-tall seven-year-old, running a finger over her uncle's Smith and Wesson Chief's Special at a family gathering. The only girl in a cluster of cousins, the only one her uncle allowed to touch his gun. "Remember, Nikoula," her uncle had said, "a gun is not good or bad—only the person who holds it. If good people don't protect us with their guns the *kleftes*, the crooks, will take over; they will run wild in the streets." Why had he told *her*—a girl—instead of the many boy cousins who were present? Had he seen how much she admired him, how she'd dreamed even then of becoming a detective like him?

A movement at the ribbon caught her eye. She snapped back to the present. A gray Chevy Caprice nosed in, and parked between two blue-and-whites. The car was familiar, sickeningly so. Dave swung from behind the wheel, big as life. He wore a nubby brown wool jacket, the soft color making his hair and eyes look darker.

She felt her heart twist into a tight knot. Why had she fallen in love with him? It was a complication she hadn't foreseen. She responded to him no matter where they were—even here at the crime scene, surrounded by cops, corpse, media. They'd tried to hide their relationship over the past year, but it was an open secret in the department. Was it the way they looked at each other? It was hard to feel that much for someone and treat him casually, like any other cop. She caught herself now, fought to control her feelings. This was no time to lose herself to emotion. She was on a case, the biggest she'd had so far.

He sighted her quickly, then looked away. Dark, angry color bloomed low on his cheeks, near his collar line. He pushed his broad-shouldered way through the crowd, waved briefly to some of the uniforms, and cleared the ribbon in a single swift motion. He nodded toward Mitchell, said "Hey, Joe!" to Stavich, bent to look at Zaporelli.

He was avoiding her. Though it was close to noon, the day seemed to have darkened. She guessed why he was angry but couldn't ask, not now, in front of everyone. He straightened and walked to where she stood. "Okay, boss," he said, "what've we got?" His cheerful tone didn't fool her. His eyes, refusing to meet hers, were focused on the lapel of her jacket.

She pointed toward Zaporelli. "I was saying he looks real neat. The car's in good shape, too, like there was no struggle." Her voice sounded peculiar, high and strained. "He must've known the perp."

"Maybe he didn't." She'd been sure Dave would oppose anything she said. If she'd announced, "The man's dead," he would have countered, "Not necessarily, could be in a coma." He indicated the body with a motion of his head. "They give you a guesstimate on when?"

"Between seven and ten last night." She envied his ability to focus on his work in spite of personal upset. That was one of the qualities that had made him a top-level homicide man, had earned him respect within the department, a reputation as an up-and-coming talent.

"What was he doing out here?" he asked.

Mitchell broke in. "He grew up around here—his mother lives a half a mile away."

Joe Stavich crushed his cigarette and dropped it into his pocket so as not to litter the crime scene. "The way I see it," he said, "he's driving along and he stops for a light. The perp comes up, knocks on the window. He rolls it down, pow!"

"What's the motive?" Dave asked. She realized from the question how much she would miss now that they weren't working together. Stavich might be competent but no one had Dave's capacity to probe. Yet given a choice, she would make the same decision again.

"The motive?" Stavich said. "Moola, what else? Who knows how much he had on him? There're creeps runnin' around would steal their grandmother's fillings out of her coffin to buy drugs." He looked toward the rows of neat houses with their little gardens. "You got the worst garbage in the world walking the streets of this city."

Nikki said, "This is still a pretty decent neighborhood—"

"Come on! I wouldn't give you two cents for *any* neighborhood in the city. Don't you read the paper?"

"The car windows are up," Nikki pointed out. "Makes me feel it happened inside. Otherwise the perp would've had to get in, roll them back up before he left. Doesn't sound like a guy who's trying to make a quick hit to buy drugs."

Meekins, the tech, had been kneeling at the side of the body. "Trakos!" His voice was low but edged with excitement. "Can you come here a minute?"

He was pointing to a second wound in the body, one none of them had noticed, a bullet hole in Zaporelli's pin-striped trousers dead center between his legs at the join of his crotch. There was little blood, a thick trickle at the site of penetration. Both the hole and blood were easy to miss against the dark navy fabric.

"Got him in the you-know-whats," Meekins said.

"The *cojones*," Stavich said.

Trencher's eyes widened. The kid's skin had a greenish cast. "Why would anyone do a thing like that?"

"Revenge," Nikki said, feeling certain of it suddenly. "That second shot came after he was dead—otherwise you'd have had a lot more blood."

"Revenge for what?" Dave challenged her.

"Who knows? Maybe he was playing around with someone's wife. Perp sent a message with that shot."

Stavich said, "You're making a big deal out of it. It's some nut who likes to perforate his victims in strange places."

Nikki didn't think so, but she said nothing.

# 2

"Could I see you a minute?" Dave asked.

She'd dreaded the question, had wanted to avoid a public scene. The techs had finished and were checking to make sure they hadn't left any equipment at the site. Stavich lit a fresh cigarette, ground the old one under his heel. Mitchell and Trencher waited near the body, ready to go through Zaporelli's pockets. Someone had brought coffee; Mitchell held his hands around a steaming container, trying to warm them.

"What is it?" Nikki said. She and Dave crossed to the unused office building at the edge of the lot, the only place there was any privacy. "I don't have much time." She'd meant it as a statement of fact but realized the minute she'd said it how uncaring it sounded.

"Don't worry. I won't take long." His anger showed openly now in the flash of his eyes. "Next time you're mad, tell me— okay? I don't have to find out from the guys on the squad. Like some schmuck who doesn't know what's going on in his own life. I come in this morning and find out the biggest case in the city went down right here in Brooklyn, *you've* got it, and you don't want *me*. A specific request."

"It's only this once." For each murder, homicide assigned a detective to the local precinct, not necessarily the same one. "For right now."

"You could've said something—"

"I didn't think I needed to—"

"Thanks a lot!"

"I didn't mean it that way," she said. "I didn't think I had to make a big deal out of it. I didn't realize you'd find out—"

"Oh, what was it? Some kind of goddamn secret?"

She'd expected him to be angry, but not this angry. "Can I talk to you?"

He scowled. "You're talking to me."

"But I don't feel as though you're listening."

"I'm listening."

"Dave, we're together all the time. We work together. At night we—"

"I thought you liked all that."

"I did. I mean, I do." Too much. That was the problem— she liked it all too much. "I need some space, a chance to—"

"Space?" His eyes narrowed, became slits. "Hey, if you want space, you can have it. Take all the space you want." His voice had risen. Stavich looked over, openly curious. Mitchell and Trencher stared carefully in the other direction. Dave said in a thick whisper, "It's what I asked you last night, isn't it?" His jaw tensed. "This is a hell of a reaction to it." He turned away, starting for his car.

"Wait a minute—" She grabbed his sleeve, but he pulled loose and strode across the lot. Had he expected her to go along with him completely last night? Fall in line with him, march obediently while he piped the tune? She would have said that, but he was well on his way to the car by now. A gust of wind rattled a wooden shutter on the office building. He ducked behind the wheel of the Chevy and drove away.

She caught the men's eyes on her. She resented Dave for putting her through this right now. All that stuff he'd said last night about caring for her—it was baloney. She'd worked with him on five murders—if he really cared for her, he wouldn't have embarrassed and upset her this way at the beginning of the biggest case she'd ever had.

Trencher slipped on a pair of rubber gloves, and went through Zaporelli's pockets. Nikki struggled to concentrate. She heard Mitchell listing the contents as though he were speaking from another planet. "Brown alligator wallet, two hundred bucks in cash, credit cards—"

Something Stavich had said clicked in her brain, and she was able to suspend her anger, focus on the case again. Stavich's theory of the random killer looking for someone to rob didn't hold up. Zaporelli still had all his valuables. "Is he wearing a watch?" she asked.

Mitchell pulled back Zaporelli's sleeve. "A beauty—a Cartier."

He handed Zaporelli's wallet and keys to her in a plastic bag. "He lived on the East Side, in the fifties. Your boss called the nineteenth to make the notification so the family wouldn't find out watching TV."

The search of the body complete, they waited for the medical examiner. Nikki kept one eye on her watch. If the M.E. didn't show up soon, the body would be taken to his office by ambulance. She said to Stavich, "I want to go see the woman who found him."

Stavich made a sound like a grunt. "I'll stay here."

She started across the lot. The sun made an appearance, peeking uncertainly through the clouds. A fishing boat lay at anchor in the bay, the *Mary J.* She remembered her mother's opposition when her father had announced Nikki would be his mate, would work on weekends and after school. "You will ruin her," her mother had warned him. "You think she is a boy? All she will be fit for is cleaning fish." Her mother had wanted her to learn the traditional skills of Greek women, ready herself for marriage. Perhaps her mother had been right—here she was at thirty-one, unmarried, still working in what was very much a man's profession.

She glanced at the gate that closed off the walkway planking. Ordinarily she enjoyed this stretch of land along Shell Bank Creek, the smell of salt air, the craft anchored in the marina; she and Dave had recently strolled along nearby Emmons Avenue to show Lara, the ten-year-old niece she was raising, where Grandpa's boat had been. But today Nikki wasn't feeling calm enough to reminisce. She had a murder to solve. Every tick of the clock gave the killer time to think up an alibi, dodge, and hide.

Celia Chaikin lived five blocks away, on Plumb 2nd. A salty wind seemed to blow Nikki most of the way, down streets so narrow that parking was permitted on only one side. She passed a boat stored for the season on a front lawn, looking bigger than the house behind it.

Most of the houses on Plumb 2nd were modest, bungalow types covered with aluminum siding. Chaikin's was the fanciest, with a fake brick facade and ornamental brass fixtures on either side of the doorway. The property was encircled by an electronic security fence; a black speaker box protruded from the gate. The lawn was sprinkled with lime, the small garden crowded with shrubs so sharply pruned they looked artificial.

Nikki pressed the buzzer on the gate. A voice crackled "Yes?" through the speaker box.

"Detective Trakos."

She heard the buzzer go off, then a dog's high yelps. A woman said soothingly, "Okay, Pippi, okay."

Pippi, a toy poodle with bows behind both ears, was under Celia Chaikin's arm when she opened the door. "Can I help you?" She was a powerfully built woman close to fifty, with dyed red hair and coarse features. She wore a violet jewel in each ear that exactly matched her expensive running suit. Her nails were lacquered in two colors, each nail divided vertically down the center in a perfect line. Through the crack of the open door Nikki glimpsed a marble entry floor and caught the scent of fresh flowers.

Nikki showed her badge, said, "Can I talk to you? I'm the case detective in the Zaporelli murder."

"Sure." On Celia's beefy hand several rings competed for attention. She bent her middle finger against her palm, rubbed it with her thumb. From inside, a man called, "Who is it?"

"A cop," Celia said. She placed the dog on the marble floor, setting off a series of yelps. "I'm handling it."

The interior of the house looked as though it had recently been remodeled, with no apparent thought to cost. The floors were pickled oak, the lights recessed to give off a soft glow, the mirrored cabinets locked to protect a collection of figurines. Nikki was examining the figures, shepherds and shepherdesses in old-fashioned dress, thinking they looked valuable, thinking the whole interior seemed too rich, out of place in this middle-income neighborhood, when the man walked into the room. He had a soft, frightened face and pasty skin. His hair had a loose flop to it, made him look unkempt.

Celia said, "Sol Chaikin, my husband."

Sol frowned but couldn't get rid of the worry in his eyes. "It's not enough my wife did the right thing, called nine one one. We have to be bothered all day?" He wore a fashionable running outfit that didn't suit him. Nikki guessed Celia chose his clothes.

Celia said, "What're you making a big deal? The officer only wants to talk to me a little. Right, officer?"

For a moment he stood his ground. "I'm just saying—"

"Go watch something, Sol. Your program's on."

He pursed his lips and retreated.

"If you want to hear about the body," Celia said to Nikki, "it happened this morning. I was walking Pippi, and he pulled me over to the car—he must've smelled something. I looked inside and almost lost last night's dinner."

"Did you recognize Zaporelli? I understand he grew up in this neighborhood."

"No."

Celia had told her husband to watch TV, but though Nikki heard the set playing distantly she could see Sol through the crack of the door. He was hiding in the next room, listening to every word. Was he concerned that Celia would say something she shouldn't, give something away? Sometimes people worried about unconnected things, like unpaid traffic tickets. The sight of a cop, any cop, made them nervous.

Celia, on the other hand, was composed. Surprisingly so for a woman who'd been upset by a dead body that morning, someone who'd "almost lost last night's dinner."

Nikki thanked her. Hesitating outside on the stoop after the door had closed, she heard the Chaikins. Sol's voice: "I told you not to call the cops!" and then an inaudible reply as the sounds moved deeper into the house. She wondered what a check on Sol and Celia Chaikin would turn up, made a note to order one.

By 1400 hours she was back at the crime scene. Midafternoon but the sun was weak, giving off a pale lemony glow with no warmth. Schoolchildren passed on their way home, gathered at the ribbon, pointed excitedly at the car, which had not yet been towed. They tried to slip past the uniforms, had to be shooed away.

"The M.E. get here?" she asked Stavich.

"Not yet."

She glanced at the body, then at her watch. "Let's roll him out of here."

An ambulance was ordered. Uniformed cops would stay with the body until it came and would wait for the tow wagon to pull out the Mercedes.

Nikki and Stavich crossed to the yellow ribbon. Off to the side a TV reporter, professionally groomed hair swept back from his forehead, stood in front of the yellow ribbon, speaking earnestly into his mike. ". . . a leader who never became pompous, no matter how high he rose. A fighter for the people. Today he has become a statistic, another victim of the rising crime rate in New York City."

A small crowd of media people stood between Nikki and the plainclothes Plymouth. One young woman with a blond Orphan Annie haircut and an open steno pad watched Nikki approach and took in her unusual height. Orphan Annie wisecracked, "You must be the big guy on the case," then signaled a photographer. Nikki saw the lens swing toward her, heard the camera click. The reporter thrust her notepad into Nikki's face and flexed her sturdy little shoulders, blocking entrance to the car. "Can you tell us what leads the police have at this point?"

It was all Nikki could do not to smack the notebook aside and lift the woman out of her way. She took a deep breath, held herself in control. After a moment good judgment and training took over. It didn't pay to antagonize the press.

"I have nothing to say right now." She pushed the mike gently aside, slid behind the steering wheel, and tried for an expression of composure. "As soon as we have something, we'll let you know."

As Nikki pulled away, she caught a glimpse of the reporter's face in the rearview mirror, glaring at her.

# 3

Rain glistened on the cables of the Brooklyn Bridge as Nikki and Stavich headed into Manhattan.

Stavich squinted up at the dark sky. "Looks like midnight and it's only four-thirty."

Lara must be home by now. Nikki had tried to call home to say she was on a murder case and wouldn't see her niece until late tonight or maybe even tomorrow morning, but the line had been busy. Nikki hated making those calls. Lara had been with her five years, ever since Nikki's sister Iris had died. She'd finally begun to make friends in the neighborhood, venture out a bit. But when Nikki was gone for long stretches Lara tended to stay close to home. Nikki had made arrangements with her landlady, Mrs. Binsey, to sit for Lara, but Binsey wasn't great company. She spent most of her time watching TV.

Stavich changed lanes with a sudden twist of the wheel, and Nikki thought for a moment the Plymouth was about to skid off the bridge.

"Practicing for your pilot's license?" she asked. He'd been weaving, tailgating, bulling his way through traffic, all the while blinded by smoke from the cigarette that dangled from the corner of his mouth, 1930s gangster-style.

He laughed. "Givin' you thrills? The wife complains, too."

Nikki decided not to watch. She opened a copy of the DD5 written four hours ago and faxed to Brooklyn by the

Manhattan detectives who had notified Zaporelli's family. She read aloud, "'Dino Zaporelli lived at—'"

"Dino?"

"That's his given name. He lived 'at 634 East 58th Street, a luxury high-rise at the corner of Third Avenue. The Zaporellis own a duplex on the sixteenth and seventeenth floors. Residents: Zaporelli's wife, Donna, and his staff manager, Elaine Lessing.'"

"What the hell's a staff manager?" Stavich asked.

She glanced up as he cut off a van on the exit ramp of the Brooklyn Bridge, jumped involuntarily as the van's side mirror came within a foot of her window. "I'm not sure," she said. "'Other help lives off the premises—maid and cook come in daily. The Zaporellis have one son, Matt, eighteen years old, living elsewhere. Neither wife nor Lessing able to furnish address.'" She paused. "That's interesting—no one knows where the son lives."

"A crock, that's what it is." He wheeled the car onto the ramp leading to the FDR Drive. The rain had slowed, leaving a high wind that buffeted the sides of the Plymouth. "The mother knows where her kid lives."

"Maybe not. When my sister Iris took off for California we didn't know where she was for a long time. She was about the same age, as a matter of fact."

"Weird," Stavich said.

"My sister was a troubled kid—maybe Zaporelli's son is, too."

"Troubled kids! Freaks and weirdos, you mean." He lit a fresh cigarette, stubbed out the old one. The air in the Fury was foul with smoke, making the skin around her eyes burn. She opened her window, felt the biting wind on her neck, rolled the glass to within an inch of the frame.

"'Zaporelli left the apartment a little before six yesterday,'" she read, "'for his regular weekly visit to his mother and sister in Brooklyn—1952 Burnett Street.' That's not far from where the body was found."

"He ever get to the mother's place?"

"We don't know yet. Someone went there to check." She held the side strap as the car swerved off the Forty-second Street exit. "Donna Zaporelli, the wife, says she was home all day yesterday. She's sick."

"What's the matter with her?"

"Rheumatoid arthritis. Her son was supposed to come, never showed."

"Where was the manager lady?"

"Lessing? She had the evening off. Says she left the house at four thirty, walked uptown on Madison, window-shopped, took the bus to Lincoln Center, saw an opera, came back to the apartment at eleven thirty."

"She got anyone to corrob that?" Stavich asked.

"No. She was alone."

He snorted. "Another crock."

Nikki folded the report and tucked it into her bag. People hurried along Third Avenue on their way home, carrying bags and packages, fighting the wind. Some held scarfs across their faces for protection. A Korean boy in a down vest, his hands red with cold, sat outside a fruit and flower store trimming roses.

They passed the corner of Forty-fifth and Third, where the Athens, Uncle Pete's coffee shop, had been. An appliance store stood in its place. Her father had worked for Uncle Pete for years while he was saving to buy his boat and had gone on working for him during the winter months when it was too cold to take the boat out.

At Fifty-fifth, three blocks from Zaporelli's address, a red, white, and blue banner in a store window caught her eye. "Zap Albany with Dean Zaporelli." In a band across the window were pictures of a smiling Zaporelli, his eyes warm, just

enough gray at his temples to inspire confidence. "Poor bastard was stuck on himself," Stavich said.

The store was in a glass-fronted complex between a haber-
dasher and a jeweler. It was dark, unoccupied. A blond woman
in very high-heeled patent-leather pumps stood at the door,
keys in hand. Stavich slowed, then stopped for a light only a
few yards away. He gave the woman his full, slit-eyed attention. She bent, inserted a key into the lock, and brushed back a
swath of silky hair falling toward her face. She worked the key,
picked up a carton that had been left in the doorway and
turned, using her back to push open the door. She was slender
and pale, her dark suit and accessories tailored to show off her
trimness. Around her neck she wore a thick gold chain that
matched oversized earrings. But what struck Nikki most were
her eyes, red-rimmed and puffy as though she'd been crying.
Nikki made a mental note to stop at the campaign office after
she'd finished with Zaporelli's wife. Something about the
svelte blonde crying outside Zaporelli's campaign office the
day after he'd been murdered intrigued her.

The lobby of Zaporelli's high-rise was crowded with uniforms, the gold-trimmed red of the building crew and the
blue of New York's finest. The cops' main job was keeping
out the army of reporters and cameramen camped outside
on the sidewalk. Satellite dishes perched on a row of news
trucks like giant black birds. An eager reporter chased Nikki
and Stavich down the circular drive and into the lobby, asking, "Did you know Zaporelli?"

Nikki shrugged him off, walked to the desk and showed
her shield to a harried young red-jacket with a self-important
air.

"The police have been here already," he said.

Nikki didn't bother to answer.

He sighed. He was only in his twenties or early thirties, but
his forehead had already set in deep ridges. "Sixteen K. The

elevator is to your right." He reached for the phone to announce them, gold epaulets shining.

The lobby was furnished like an emir's palace, damask draperies, balloon-shade lamps, Oriental carpets. More red-jackets met them, accompanied them to the elevator, made sure they were comfortable, pressed floor buttons, and sent them on their way. Nikki expected one of them to say bon voyage.

The elevator slid noiselessly upward and stopped on the sixteenth floor. With a well-greased glide the doors opened into a mirrored entry foyer shared by two apartments. A mural had been etched on the glass—a rocky outcrop over-looking a bay. A boy sat on the topmost rock, studying the water. The mural made Nikki remember the stories her father had told of his boyhood, how he'd stared at the Aegean, dreamed of coming to America.

A small gray-haired woman with a worried look answered the chime. She glanced past Nikki toward Stavich. "Detective Trakos?"

"*I'm* Detective Trakos," Nikki said. "This is Detective Stavich."

Her eyes were younger than the rest of her, brown and lively. "I'm Elaine Lessing," she said. She motioned them in.

The staff manager. Nikki judged her to be about sixty, with the energy of someone half her age. She wore a blue knit suit with white trim at the collar and cuffs, low-heeled shoes, no jewelry except for small gold hoop earrings. She looked at Stavich uncertainly, her nose lifting as though she sniffed something noxious. Nikki, standing next to him, real-ized he smelled of stale tobacco. His clothes were saturated with the odor because of his nonstop smoking. She suddenly remembered the cigarette he'd dumped into his pocket at the crime scene—had he forgotten to take it out?

Lessing led them into a good-sized vestibule. The red car-pet with the gold medallion at the center looked expensive, the carved cherry-wood desk genuinely old. A phone rang in a distant room. Lessing said, "Excuse me a minute," and hurried out.

Stavich looked down the three steps ahead of them, into the sunken living room with its wraparound view of the East River. "This fancy crap gets on my nerves."

"Not exactly what I'm used to either."

A pink marble fireplace graced the side wall of the living room. Nikki wondered whether it was ever used, and if so, where the smoke went. Up to the second floor of the duplex? Or was it channeled ingeniously and expensively outside? An assortment of frames jostled for room on the mantel, a wedding photo at the center, the bride nestled lovingly against the groom. Without warning Nikki was thrown back to last night in Dave's apartment, to his proposal. "I want to marry you." It had been just like him, nothing subtle about it. They'd gotten out of bed. She was dressing, getting ready to go home. "I want to marry you. I never felt this way about anyone before. What're we waiting for? We're not kids."

Her first reaction had been joy. She'd felt as though her heart had taken off and was dancing someplace out in the night sky, over the rooftops. But her initial happiness gave way to uncertainty as she considered his proposal.

Their relationship was fun now, carefree. If they married, things would change. She pictured her parents' home, the homes of her aunts and uncles. There had been shining waxed floors, a hot meal on the table every night. Her career mattered to her. So did marriage. She just didn't know if she could do justice to both. She needed time away from Dave to think.

She tugged herself back to the present as Elaine Lessing returned. "I'd like to speak with Mrs. Zaporelli," Nikki said.

She frowned. "She isn't well. Do you have to question her—she just came back from identifying the body. We've had police here all day, going through everything."

"I have to talk to everyone involved, even if you've been questioned before."

"But we—"

"Mrs. Lessing—"

"Miss."

"Miss Lessing, it'll take less time if you cooperate."

The skin on her forehead wrinkled like parchment, and she blinked. "I'm just trying to keep her well. You have no idea what this trip to the morgue cost her. Her doctor said she should rest."

She seemed weighed down by responsibility, as though she alone had to safeguard Donna Zaporelli's health. Nikki had a twinge of guilt that she was adding to Elaine Lessing's burden, then remembered the corpse slumped against the side of the Mercedes. His wife could be made uncomfortable for a while if it meant discovering who had killed him.

They followed Elaine Lessing up an oak staircase. A large open space narrowed into a corridor off which several rooms opened. They passed a tailored bedroom with a mahogany armoire and bedposts, a valet stand holding a satin-lapeled dinner suit. Zaporelli's bedroom? Had he and his wife slept in separate rooms? There was no law against it, but voices from Nikki's childhood chattered in Greek that sleeping apart meant more than just a physical separation. She remembered when her father had had pneumonia the doctor had wanted her mother to sleep on the living room sofa for a week. "Sophia," Nikki's grandmother had urged her, "do not leave your husband's bed. God will watch over you, keep you well."

At the end of the hall, two doors stood open. One was an office, with filing cabinets, shelves, and computer setup. From the open door next to it a woman's voice tumbled, high and agitated. "Glenn's not there? What do you mean—he works there, doesn't he? . . . think Matt would've called to let me know he's all right. I don't understand why he hasn't called. You tell that to Glenn when you see him."

Elaine Lessing's eyes widened anxiously. "Wait here, please," she said, and raced in the direction of the voice.

The woman went on, getting louder, a twist of terror making her voice shrill. "Tell him I'm out of my mind with worry. I don't like the way he looked. He—" There was an abrupt silence, as though Lessing had signaled her. Then, barely audible, "Let me know if he —" Nikki heard the receiver drop into its cradle. Then, accusingly, in a fierce whisper, "You should have told me they were here! You always do this, let people walk in on me!"

Elaine Lessing scurried back to them. This half-run was her ordinary pace, Nikki suspected, as though she were late for something. "Mrs. Zaporelli will see you now. Remember, not a second longer than you have to."

Stavich took out his Camels and lighter, but before he could pull out a cigarette Elaine Lessing said, "You can't smoke in the house." She blinked, trying to look determined.

"How about downstairs?" Stavich said.

"Nowhere in the apartment. It isn't good for Mrs. Z." He set his lips hard, slipped the cigarettes back into his pocket. "Sorry," she said, blinking again.

She went next door to the office. Had she placed herself there so she could hear them? Or to protect Zaporelli's wife from their rubber hoses?

Donna Zaporelli lay propped on pillows under the canopy of a draped bed frame. The room's decorations seemed to reflect her. They were handsome but faded, as though they'd both been formed in another time and were having trouble keeping up. Dark, almost black hair framed her silken olive skin and large eyes. "Sit down." She'd been beautiful, maybe as recently as ten years ago in her twenties, but she was too well fleshed now, and a silver thread gleamed here and there above her ears. Lines of weariness dragged from nose to mouth. Gravity, or maybe trouble, had pulled her down, aged her. She turned her head to indicate chairs on either side of

the bed but winced before she'd completed the motion. "I didn't figure they'd send more cops. They had a whole army here before. They went through his room." Her speech carried a strong Brooklyn-Italian flavor; she said "ditn't" for "didn't." She spoke with her hands. It seemed out of place in the elegant duplex. As though aware of that, she tried to curb the movements of her fingers, one hand holding the other like a captured bird. "I'd see you down in the living room, but I'm sick—rheumatoid arthritis. Gets worse when I'm stressed."

On an oversize nightstand at the side of the bed a cluster of frames held pictures of a boy at various ages, the most recent in his late teens. He resembled Zaporelli, dark Roman eyes and classic features. Nikki guessed it must be his son, Matt. He was better looking than his father, but he had an angry, defiant expression Zaporelli hadn't had. There wasn't a single photo of Zaporelli himself. Had the widow hidden his pictures when she'd learned of his death, not wanting to remind herself of her loss? Or had her husband's pictures never had that intimate a place, near her bed? On the opposite nightstand a collection of prescription pill bottles, tubes, and creams spilled on to a tray. The air had a close sickroom smell.

Nikki sat on one side of the bed, Stavich opposite. "Mrs. Zaporelli," Nikki said, "can you tell me when you last saw your husband?" She took a steno book from her purse, clicked open a ballpoint pen.

"I answered that question already—the other cops asked the same thing."

"Sorry to make you go through it again," Nikki said. "What did you tell them?"

Her gaze went flat with impatience. "I saw him yesterday. He came back from campaign headquarters about three."

"Headquarters—that's the place three blocks away?"

"Yeah. He stayed here a coupla hours. He didn't have dinner. He always goes to his mother's Tuesday."

"He went to his mother's by himself?"

Something changed in her face, adding to the droop of her cheeks. "Yeah. The trip's too much for me." She said it without conviction.

"The time you spent together," Nikki said. "Who else was here?"

The slightest hesitation. "No one—just me and Dean. Elaine had the evening off. The cook was gone for the day." Her irises were soft brown, the color of honey, of sunny childhood innocence. Looking closer, Nikki saw shrewdness and calculation behind them. "You have a maid?"

"Three times a week. Tuesday isn't one of her days."

"Did you and your husband talk about anything special?"

There was a flash of fear in her eyes. "No. The usual."

"Which was?"

"His announcement party. It was gonna be this Thursday, at the Hyatt. The mayor had just accepted—he was happy about that. He wanted to know if Elaine called the catering chief. I said I didn't know."

"What else?"

Fear now flickered openly across her face. "Nothing."

Nikki caught Stavich's glance across the bed, his disbelieving look. She paused and let the silence gather weight, a technique she used when she thought someone was hiding information. She scribbled meaningless words into her notebook, turned a few pages, the rattle of the paper loud in the room. The phone rang and was answered by Elaine Lessing in the adjoining room. "Zaporelli residence. Sorry, she's not taking any calls." Nikki let the seconds stretch to a full minute. When she thought she'd waited long enough to throw Donna Zaporelli off balance she said, "How would you describe your relationship with your husband?"

"What has that got to do with anything?"

"We have to know."

The full chin softened, almost quivered. "He was—we

tried not to get in each other's way. As far as being a couple—going out, doing things—we didn't. Not anymore." A
tear collected at the corner of each eye. She tried to reach
for a tissue on the nightstand, frowned at the pain, settled
back against the pillows. She lifted her hand, slowly and carefully, brushed at her eyes. "We didn't even do political stuff
anymore. You know, places where he had to put in an
appearance or make a speech."

"You can't get out much?" Nikki asked gently.

"I can. It's just—Most days I have to use an ugly cane."
Nikki followed her glance to the stick leaning against the far
side of the nightstand. It was an intricately crafted piece,
carved and inset with stones, not ugly at all. Nikki was suddenly aware of how much attention the woman paid to her
appearance in spite of her illness. Her robe was fashionable,
her hair professionally groomed. Diamonds sparkled from several fingers and were set into the lobe of each ear. "He said I
didn't look—" She swallowed hard, letting her tears flow freely
now, running down her cheeks in two wet tracks. "He said the
way I looked, it was bad for his *image.*" Hate spewed out with
the word. She sucked in her lip as if to call it back.

"How did you feel about that?"

"He was dead wrong—I was his wife! Did Bush dump
Barbara when she got sick? Did Gerald Ford? But with
Dean . . . everything had to be perfect." Her shoulders
slumped as though tired of fighting. "That's how he was. I
just had to accept it." She didn't sound as if she had.

"It's tough to live with something like that," Nikki said.

"Yeah." Her eyes narrowed suddenly. "Hey, wait a
minute. What're you getting at? That it bugged me so much I
got him killed? No way! I wanted to lots of times, but that's
different. We went our separate ways. We weren't the only
couple in New York doing that, you know."

An established arrangement, sanctioned by time. Donna
Zaporelli seemed hurt and disappointed, but Nikki had to

agree—the fading of the original relationship wouldn't have made her angry enough to murder. Not unless she'd been given added cause.

"Mrs. Zaporelli, what did you do after your husband left?"

"Nothing. Tried to watch TV, but I kept falling asleep."

"You didn't go out?"

"No. It was one of my bad days."

"Was anyone else here?"

"After Dean left? No. Elaine came in about eleven." She glanced at a jewel-studded watch. "You almost through?"

Nikki looked at the DD5 report. "It says here you have a son."

The words had a noticeable effect. She stiffened against the pillow, became more alert. "That's right. Why're you asking about him?"

"We check everyone close to the victim."

"But Matty didn't live here."

"He saw his father, didn't he?"

"Not that often."

"How often?"

"Let's see. Once a month, maybe." Her face was smooth, unreadable. She looked less the invalid; her wariness had strengthened her.

Nikki said, "Your son was supposed to come here yesterday."

"Yes, but he didn't. In fact, I'm worried about him. He always shows up when he says he's coming and this time he didn't. He shoulda called—if he's not coming, that's what he usually does. I waited all day, but I didn't see or hear from him." She was babbling now, piling word on word to build a wall of defense. Nikki remembered the frantic sound in her voice before Elaine Lessing had shushed her. She'd been talking to someone, asking them to tell someone named Glenn how worried she was—she hadn't liked "the way he looked." If that was her son she'd been talking about, then she *had* seen him. Looking at her now, at the steely determination under the soft exterior, Nikki realized that if it were true, she would never get the woman to admit it.

"Where can I reach Matt?" Nikki asked.

"I wish I knew, I'd call him myself." Nikki believed her—she looked worried enough to be telling the truth. Nikki glanced again at the photo of the angry young man. His hair was loose and long, fell in dark waves to his shoulders. An earring shone in the lobe of one ear. He wore a T-shirt from ACT UP, the AIDS activist organization, and jeans torn at the knee.

Donna said, "He moved out last year—he was having a hard time."

"With your husband?"

"With *both* of us," she stated firmly. "He didn't give us his address."

"Or a phone number?"

"No."

Stavich frowned. Nikki could almost hear him say, *What a crock!*

"What was the fight about?" Nikki asked.

"Oh, for God's sake! What has the fight got to do with Dean's murder? I don't *remember* what it was about. It was too long ago!"

Her voice had risen like an alarm. As though in answer to it Elaine Lessing ran back into the room. "You're making her sick!" she said to Nikki, her eyes blinking rapidly. She placed herself in front of Donna like a shield. "Her husband died less than twenty-four hours ago—she just came from the Medical Examiner's—and you're putting her through a third degree! Where's your compassion?" Without waiting for an answer she turned and bent her gray head close to the widow's. "Are you okay, Donna?"

"No, I'm not! How much do I have to put up with? I oughta call the Commissioner and find out."

Nikki hesitated. She could insist on her right to continue questioning. But Donna obviously had friends in high places. A call to the Commissioner would set off a chain reaction that would end with Eagle-Eye summoning her to his office, maybe even taking her off the case. It was a hassle she didn't need. She said, "I'll be another minute. I can hold some questions for another time, but there are things I need to ask now."

"Such as?" Elaine cut in.

Nikki stood, moved past her to the foot of the bed. "Did he have any enemies you knew of?" she asked Donna.

"I can't think of any. You mean political?"

"Any kind."

"No. He was popular." She said it with reluctant admiration, as though it pained her to admit any positive qualities in him.

"No unhappy employees, anything like that?"

"Not that I know of."

Nikki turned to Elaine. "Can *you* think of anyone? Maybe someone he offended."

"Not offhand."

"No threatening notes or phone calls?"

"No."

Stavich stood and said, "Excuse me. Could I use your bathroom?"

Donna didn't look thrilled, but she pointed to a door in the corner.

Nikki went on with her questions, not waiting for him. "Did Mr. Zaporelli own a gun?"

Donna's forehead wrinkled. "A gun?"

Elaine said, "He bought a revolver a few weeks ago."

Donna frowned. "Why didn't you tell me?"

Elaine said hesitantly, "It didn't seem to have anything to do with you—"

"To *do* with me? What's wrong with you? My husband buys a gun and it has nothing to *do* with me?"

"He told me he'd be down at headquarters all kinds of hours, and he didn't like walking home alone in the dark."

"That's ridiculous," Donna said. "Three blocks? Besides, he never was afraid before."

"The city's getting tougher," Elaine said. "I know I'm scared every time *I* go out. Maybe he *was* frightened."

"Maybe of someone in particular," Nikki said.

# 4

"He bought the gun at the beginning of March," Elaine said.

"He kept it at headquarters?" Nikki asked.

"No, here, in the office. I saw it a few days ago."

"Is it still here?"

"I'll check." She left her post at the side of Donna's bed and went into the office. Nikki followed, watched her pull out the top drawer of a file cabinet. Her figure was girlish and trim, in surprising contrast to her gray head. There wasn't an extra bulge under the blue knit, though Nikki detected the shaping of a girdle. It was mostly in her face that her age showed, the loose folds of flesh around her cheeks and throat, the deep pouches under her eyes. She searched in the drawer, reached and rummaged behind the files. She frowned, fine lines creasing her forehead. "It's gone. Was he killed with his own gun?"

"We don't know. We're checking."

"Here's the paperwork." She handed Nikki a folder.

It was all in order—a copy of the application for the permit to carry, a pistol license issued by the city, a receipt from the International Arms Corporation on Fifth Avenue, licensed gun dealers. He had charged a .38 Colt to his MasterCard. The gun in the glove compartment had been a .38 Colt. "Can I take these?" Nikki asked.

"Let me copy them first."

She fed the papers into a desk copier. Stavich shuffled back in and Nikki told him, "He had a gun," indicating the papers with a motion of her head. Stavich nodded. He didn't seem surprised or unsurprised; his face showed no emotion.

The phone rang again. Elaine grabbed it, said hello, then looked disappointed. "No, she's not taking calls." And yet Donna *had* taken a call, had been on the phone and mentioned Glenn, whoever that was, when Nikki had waited outside her room. Elaine said, "Thanks, I'll tell her," replaced the receiver and went back to copying. If Donna wasn't taking calls, why didn't Elaine use the answering machine on the desk? Unless she or Donna were expecting a call they *would* take. She remembered Donna saying, "Let me know if he —"

She glanced idly at the collection of framed certificates and diplomas on the walls, all Zaporelli's. He'd received an award for underwriting Hope for the Homeless, a benefit concert. He'd graduated from Brown University twenty years ago, with a Bachelor of Arts degree. He'd been a member of Sock and Buskin, Brown's theatrical society. Last year he'd donated generously to the Brown Alumni Association, had been named a Benefactor.

She looked around again, studied the room in a different light. The space was Elaine's—the desk had a black and brass stand that said ELAINE LESSING, STAFF MANAGER—yet there wasn't a single personal item in it. Not a picture or plaque, no gimmicky items on the desk. Aside from the name stand, a calendar and the answering machine, the desk was bare.

"How long have you worked for Mr. Zaporelli?" Nikki asked.

"Five years. I was a volunteer at district headquarters and he offered me a job."

"Doing what?"

"Typing and filing. He had an office on lower Broadway that handled his legal stuff. When he decided to run for Council, he cut back on his practice. He closed the office, let people go. I figured I'd be cut and was getting ready to leave when he asked me if I'd work here. Mrs. Z was getting sicker, and he wanted to know if I'd be willing to live here and help her, do some secretarial work for him in my spare time. I'd never done anything but office work, and I wasn't sure. I told him I'd think about it." She collected the copies, shuffled them into a neat pile. "I'm not sorry. It really worked out. At my age where would I ever have found a job like this?" Her glance took in the carpeted office and modern equipment. Her eyes misted. "Whatever he was, he was good to me."

"Whatever he was?" Nikki said.

She looked suddenly more alert, on her guard. She blinked rapidly. "I mean . . . everyone has faults. Everybody." She turned her attention to the copies in her hand. Nikki waited for her to go on, but she set her mouth tightly. She dug in her drawer, concentrated on finding the perfect paper clip to hold the papers. Nikki decided not to pursue the subject of Zaporelli's faults. What was it her mother used to say when Nikki went at things head-on? "Ten small strokes are better than one big one." "You were out last night," Nikki said.

"I went to the opera."

"What did you see?"

The dark squirrel-eyes opened wider, puzzled. Nikki assured her, "It's just for the record."

"Oh. Thomas Hampson in *The Barber—The Barber of Seville.*"

Nikki scribbled, not sure how to spell the names, tilted her pad so Elaine wouldn't see. She would have to look up the names in the newspaper when she wrote her report. "Was it good?"

"Oh yes. He's great, Hampson. A really magnificent voice."

In the background she could see the smirk on Stavich's face. She herself had never been around opera enough to know or enjoy it.

"When did you leave here?"

"About four thirty."

"And you got home at—"

"Eleven."

"By cab?"

"No. I hate taking cabs—you never know who's behind the wheel. Car service."

Elaine clipped the papers together, receipt on top, and handed them over. Nikki was about to slip them into her purse when the receipt caught her attention. She read it carefully, then asked, "How come your boss didn't buy bullets?"

Elaine blinked. "Let me see that again." She slipped on a pair of half-glasses and glanced at the receipt. "I never noticed before."

"He coulda bought the bullets in Jersey," Stavich said. "They're cheaper there."

"The money wouldn't have mattered to him," Elaine said, sounding snippy. "Why would he buy a gun in New York, then run over to Jersey to buy bullets?"

"You're right," Nikki said. "It doesn't make sense." She folded the papers into her purse as they trooped back to the bedroom.

Donna lay against the pillows almost exactly as they'd left her. Her skin seemed paler, drained of life. "Are you through?" she asked.

"A few loose ends. Where did your husband go when he left the apartment—where did he park his car?"

"In the garage under the building. Why do I have to be bothered with that kind of question? Elaine could have told you."

"Would he reach the garage through the lobby?"

"No. There's an entrance on the basement level, off the elevator. What else do you want to know? Where the elevator is? Exactly how many times he pressed the button?"

Ignoring her, Nikki made a big production of searching

through her notebook, saying finally, "I guess that's it." She moved slowly to the door, conscious of the look that crossed Donna's face, relief so strong Nikki could almost touch it. At the door she turned. "There is one thing, Mrs. Zaporelli. Who is Glenn?"

Donna's skin went from olive to sickly yellow. "What're you trying to do—rip my guts apart? Is that what you want?"

Elaine looked as though she'd been bitten by her pet dog. "I thought you weren't going to upset her!"

Donna shouted, "Glenn has nothing to do with this!"

"Then why not tell me who he is?"

"Where'd you hear about him?"

"Who is he, Mrs. Zaporelli?"

Donna's glance went from Nikki to Stavich, then back again, as she searched for an answer to her predicament.

"If you don't tell me," Nikki said, "I'll find out anyhow. We'll keep—"

"He's my son's roommate. Or was. I don't know for sure because Matty won't tell me *where* he's living, but I think they're still together."

"Where can I reach Glenn?"

"All I have is the number of his supervisor. He works at Bellevue as a medic."

"What's his full name?"

"Glenn Taylor." She spelled it, closed her eyes against a sudden pain, sank back on the pillows. "Will you get *out* of here?"

Elaine's eyebrows arched up, two anxious curves. She whispered, "She'll need a week to recover from this."

"We're through," Nikki said.

Elaine turned to Donna. "Take it easy, okay? I'll show them out and come right back."

Donna didn't answer. Eyes closed, she lay in a private world of pain. Or was she faking it for their benefit? It was hard to tell.

At top speed Elaine led them through the hall, down the steps and out to the elevator. "I'm sorry," she said breathlessly. Nikki guessed she couldn't wait to race back to Donna's side.

In the elevator Stavich said, "So whaddaya think—did Florence Nightingale knock off her boss, or did the ever-lovin' wife do him?" He pulled a Camel from his pack, lit it, filled the car with smoke. "My money's on the missus."

"What'd you find out in the bathroom?"

He handed Nikki a piece of paper. "That's her doctor's number—name's Fishberg. I got it off her pills. She's sick, she can't walk, she's a cripple, right? I wanna hear what he says about her."

# 5

The young red-jacket with the ridged forehead was on duty as Nikki and Stavich came through the lobby. He was talking on the phone. His eyes seemed to widen as he caught sight of them. He kept his glance on them, appearing even more worried as he whispered into the receiver. As Nikki headed in his direction he hung up, grabbed a black ledger and disappeared into a room just behind the desk.

He came back a minute later, laid the book down, and said stiffly, "How may I help you?"

Nikki said, "You can tell me if you keep a record of who goes in and out."

"A record of visitors? Of course." He turned the black-bound book so it faced her and pulled back the front cover. "A complete list." He pointed. "When the person came, their name, what apartment they were visiting, when they left."

The only pages in the book were today's sheets, labeled March 25 at the top, a dozen blank ones under them. It was the kind of book that opened with a key, for easy removal or addition of pages. Red-jacket lifted the top two sheets, pointed a manicured nail toward the line that read, *Det. Nikki Trakos, 3:58 P.M., 16K.* "You see—everyone gets listed. If I don't list you, you don't come in—unless you're a tenant."

"Where are yesterday's sheets?"

Something tensed behind his glance. "Yesterday's? We don't keep the old ones."

"Isn't that unusual?" Nikki asked. "What's the point of this kind of record if you don't hold onto it?"

His jaw jutted stubbornly. "I just take orders."

Nikki remembered he'd been on the phone right before he'd run into the back room with the book. "*Who* are you taking orders *from?*"

"What do you mean?" A line of sweat beaded his upper lip and spread to his cheeks as though the temperature in the lobby had climbed ten degrees.

Stavich said, "It's a criminal offense to hold back evidence in a murder case."

The ridges on Red-jacket's forehead deepened. "I don't have the sheets. They went out with yesterday's trash."

"If it comes right down to it, a grand jury can subpoena those sheets," Stavich said.

A droplet of sweat descended from Red-jacket's temple and fell on the gold epaulet. "I don't know what you're talking about."

Nikki asked, "Were you on duty yesterday?"

"Yes."

"I guess we'll have to rely on your memory, then. Who went in or out of the Zaporellis' apartment?"

"It was fairly quiet. Mr. Zaporelli left early, at about nine, didn't come back till about three. The cook left at four, Miss Lessing at four thirty. I didn't see Mr. Zaporelli leave, so I assume he went through the garage."

Nikki said pointedly, "Of course if you only have your memory to go by . . ."

Red-jacket gave her a look of total hatred.

"Is this the only way out of the building," she asked, "besides the garage?"

"No, there's the basement entrance."

"Can we see that?"

He banged his palm on a metal dome that made a bell sound. "One of the staff will show you."

"We'll be back later," she said. "Maybe you'll remember more."

"Yeah," Stavich put in. "Maybe you'll remember where you put the sheets."

They stepped away from the desk. Nikki could feel Red-jacket's anger like a vibration behind them.

Stavich said, "The wife must've called down right after we left and told him to get rid of the pages. What's she trying to hide?"

"Not what," Nikki said. "*Who*." She remembered the pictures of Matt Zaporelli crowding the nightstand near Donna's bed, how the woman had babbled compulsively when Nikki had asked if she'd seen her son the day before. "I waited all day," she'd said, "but I didn't see or hear from him."

They stepped out of the elevator on the basement level, following the red-jacket assigned to them down a cinder-block corridor. On the right was a laundry room where one of the dryer drums rotated noisily. Opposite, a locked storage room.

Stavich said to the red-jacket, an older man with dyed brown sideburns, "Any security down here?"

"Suppose to be here, you can never find 'im."

Nikki glanced toward the end of the corridor. "That door locked?"

"From outside. You want to go out, you push it open and it locks behind you."

She said to Stavich as they walked back to the elevator, "So if the wife wanted to, she could've gone out this way."

He lit a fresh Camel. "Coulda took her cane and went for a stroll. No one woulda seen her."

There was a pay phone against the whitewashed wall of the garage, opposite the elevator. Nikki was alone. Stavich had gone to Bellevue to talk to Glenn Taylor, Matt Zaporelli's roommate. He would meet her later at the station house. Dritzer, the Borough Chief, was expected at six for a conference on the case.

She dialed home.

"Hello?" Lara sounded preoccupied.

"It's Mom." Three months ago Lara had asked Nikki if she could call her Mom instead of Aunt Nikki. Nikki still hadn't gotten used to it.

"Honey, I'll be home late tonight." She felt as though she had a daily pill to swallow, a ration of guilt—for being a working parent, for loving her job, for being away from home as much as she was. Lara knew by now what a murder case meant days of not seeing Nikki, lonely evenings, bedtimes without a good-night kiss. She still read to Lara at night, from the *Greek Myths and Legends* book Nikki'd had since childhood. She kept expecting Lara to announce that she was too grown-up for a bedtime story, but so far that hadn't happened.

"I'm on a murder case again."

"I heard about it," Lara said. "Uncle Dave told me."

"He called?"

"A little while ago. He'll be over later for a cooking lesson." In his spare time Dave had been teaching Lara to cook. Nikki had a sudden, irrational urge to tell Lara she shouldn't let him come over, that he was being kept at a distance, shouldn't be part of the family unless and until Nikki made a decision about him. Then she realized Lara didn't need space from Dave— only Nikki did. Lara had already made up her mind. With all the purity of her ten-year-old heart she loved him more than any other man she knew, more even than Nikki's father.

Lara said now, "We're going to make a quiche."

"Oh."

"Didn't he tell you?"

Nikki hesitated, thought of her last conversation with Dave, their angry exchange at the crime scene. "No."

"Did you two have a fight?" Lara asked anxiously.

"Not really. We just—"

"Then how come you didn't know he was coming over later?"

"I guess he didn't tell me." Why was it so easy for Lara to put her on the defensive when they talked about Dave? "Lara, it isn't really your business."

A pause. "Okay."

"It's between me and Uncle Dave."

"What happened?"

"Lara!"

"O-*kay!*"

"I don't mean to hurt your feelings," Nikki said, "but you shouldn't be so involved."

"I'm not hurt. I just wanted to know."

Ten years old, going on thirty. "I'll try to get home in time to say good night," Nikki said.

She held the phone for minutes after Lara had hung up, feeling grateful that Dave hadn't allowed his anger with her to overflow onto Lara. Impulsively, she dialed his number.

"Homicide, Lawton."

"It's me," she said. "Thanks for going over to see Lara later. I wasn't sure you would."

"Okay."

She couldn't tell his mood from the sound of his voice, the single word. "You still angry?"

"Not as much."

"I should've talked to you before I got a new partner. I'm sorry."

"Accepted. When am I going to see you?"

"I don't know. I meant what I said about needing time to think. Especially now, with the case. My brain's on overload."

A pause, then, "Okay. See you around."

She hung up, dissatisfied with the way the conversation had ended.

She found the garage manager in his office. A thin, light-skinned Haitian, he told her in cheerful tones that he kept only the current day's records of cars pulling in and out. Yes, he'd seen Mr. Zaporelli yesterday—he'd had Mr. Zaporelli's car brought out at five thirty. He had a standing order for that time every Tuesday.

"Who was with him when he left?"

"He was alone."

"During the day, did anyone come in to see the Zaporellis?"

His glance slid toward the phone on his desk. "No," he said. "Nobody."

Donna had been thorough.

Nikki wondered whether to go upstairs again, accuse Donna of hiding information, force her to reveal what the big cover-up was about. She decided against it.

A too-thin woman with a short page boy got off the elevator, said hello to the garage manager and waited near the glassed-in office. She wore a blazer and carried an alligator-skin bag. Nikki had the urge to question her, then remembered Eagle-Eye had ordered a canvass of the building— every tenant would be questioned.

An attendant drove a BMW to the office. He held the door for the woman. When she'd gone, he leaned into the office and checked something on a clipboard, his carrot-colored hair brighter under the sharp light. He turned, then walked back toward the rows of cars.

Nikki thanked the manager.

"That's all right. Anything we can do."

She headed for the elevator. She heard noise below her and realized there was at least another level to the garage. She found a staircase, slipped inside quietly, and eased down the steps sideways, so her high heels wouldn't click against the metal.

The lower level was just like the upper one except that it

had no office. The orange-haired attendant was bent over the hood of a maroon Cadillac, his hair clashing with the color of the car. He glanced up as she approached. "Help you?"

She showed her ID.

He straightened, wiped his hands on his coveralls. "My name's MacFadden, Tom MacFadden."

He was young, no more than twenty-five, his upturned nose and freckles making him look boyish.

"Were you down here yesterday, about five thirty, six o'clock?" Instinctively, she kept her voice low.

MacFadden glanced at the staircase. "If you mean did I see Mr. Zaporelli then, I did. He came running in, got into his car, took off."

"Did you talk to him?"

"I tried to. I called over—he was parked right there." He pointed to the corner. "He always said, 'How're you doing, Tommy?' or asked me how things were going. But he didn't even hear me yesterday. He slammed the door so hard I thought he'd break the window." He started to say something else, changed his mind.

"Is there more?" Nikki prompted.

"Well, it's just . . . he was alone. Every other Tuesday Miss Royce was with him—the lady who runs his campaign office."

Nikki remembered the teary blonde in the doorway of Zaporelli's headquarters. "Tall, good-looking, long blond hair?" Nikki held her hand at her shoulder to estimate the length of hair.

"That's her. She'd come here early on Tuesdays, about four fifteen, and wait for him upstairs. They'd drive out together. Yesterday she didn't show."

"No one was with him?"

"Not when *I* saw him."

Nikki pulled her book out of her purse and made some notes. "What kind of man was he?"

"Mr. Zaporelli?" MacFadden hesitated. "I didn't know him well. I mean he tipped me and gave me a decent present at Christmas, but otherwise I didn't have much to do with him—we never really talked." He swallowed, his Adam's apple bobbing above the red collar. "Most of what I know I heard from his son—he talked about him a lot."

"Matt?"

"His friends call him Matty."

"Are you his friend?"

He thought for a moment. "I guess. I know him a long time, since I started work here five years ago. He was just a kid then, twelve, thirteen years old. A lot of nights when I was alone he'd come down to get out of the house—he didn't get along with his folks. We'd sit and talk, have a—a smoke together."

Nikki suspected he'd been going to say "joint" instead of "smoke" and had remembered at the last minute she was a cop. "What kinds of things did you talk about?"

"His singing. He wants to do it professionally, be a big star. His heart's set on it, has been ever since I met him. He used to gripe to me that his father was dead against it. He was going to do it anyway, he said. We used to talk music a lot. We were both into heavy metal. He'd bring down his tapes and we'd play them. A while ago—it was after he moved out—I went to hear him sing at this place in the Village, the Blue Boy. His roommate came too."

"Glenn?"

"Yeah. An okay guy. I mean they're both—they're gay. That doesn't bother me. I even brought my girlfriend along—I think we were the only straight people there."

Nikki jotted down MacFadden's name and some notes on what he'd said. "How did Matty feel about his father?"

He picked up a polishing cloth, shook it open, and folded it again. "Like I told you—they had a lot of arguments."

"About?"

"Money. Matty said there was money coming to him, but his father wouldn't let him have it."

"Why not?"

"He wanted Matty to get a job or go to school, give up singing."

Nikki closed her notebook, slipping her pen back into her purse.

"Can I ask you a question?" MacFadden said. "Is Matty in trouble?"

"What makes you ask?"

"Well, basically he's a good kid. But he was crazy yesterday—steamed up. I haven't seen him like that in a long time."

"He was *here* yesterday?"

"Yeah, twice. Once in the afternoon, and then I thought I saw him last night—once about seven and then about eight thirty. At least I thought it was him. He was across the street—I called him, but he ran away."

"Tell me about the first time, in the afternoon."

"He came down about ten minutes before his father. He was mad as hell. He had a bruise the size of an egg on his jaw—said his father socked him. I told him to get some ice on it, but he didn't hear me. He kept saying, 'I'm gonna kill that son of a bitch!' I tried to get him to sit down and cool off, but he wouldn't listen. He just ran out. He didn't mean anything—it's the kind of thing people say all the time."

But some of the freckles on MacFadden's forehead disappeared as he frowned. It gave him a worried, less boyish look.

# 6
---

Karen Royce was the only one in the campaign office when Nikki pulled up at five. Should she stop and interview the woman? If she did, she'd be late for the conference at the station house. She had a momentary image of Eagle-Eye's angry face, but then a car pulled out of a spot in front of the office; she took this as a sign that the interview was meant to be. She parked and had to fight the wind as she got out of the car. She knocked on the glass door.

Karen had been holding her head in her hands so that her hair dipped toward the desk lamp, shining gold under the light. She looked up, saw Nikki at the locked door, and waved her hands back and forth to show the office was closed. Nikki opened her ID case, flattening it against the glass. Karen rose, crossed the carpet in stockinged feet, read the ID, and reached down to turn the lock. Her legs and feet were shapely inside sheer nylon, her toenails painted.

"Miss Royce?"

She nodded. She lifted her hair on either side of her head with the middle finger of each hand, tucked her hair behind her ears. She had pretty ears, small and delicate, like pink seashells. She led Nikki back to the desk without a word, pointed wearily to a seat, slumped into her chair. Her eyes were filled with sorrow—the sorrow of loss, or of remorse? Nikki wasn't sure, but the woman's suffering was clear, her grief close to the surface. On her desk was a cup, an opened can of tomato juice, a bottle of Worcestershire sauce. Nikki thought back to Uncle Chris, who'd had a tendency to drink too much at weddings. The next morning Aunt Katina would make him a concoction of the same ingredients for his hangover. Karen followed Nikki's glance toward the cup and said in low, shaky tones, "I have a virus." She seemed younger than she had from a distance. She'd chosen clothing that made her look sophisticated, competent, but her manner was unsure. It made Nikki think of a girl dressed in her mother's things.

"Sorry you haven't been feeling well," Nikki said.

Karen lifted the drink, her hand trembling, and sipped. A chunky gold bracelet slid toward her wrist, making it appear fragile, though her hands looked strong and capable. She wore a gold ring on her middle finger in the shape of her initial, "K."

Except for the slosh of liquid in Karen's cup, the office was completely silent. From a stack of posters on the floor, the same as those in the window, Zaporelli smiled up at the fluorescent light. At the next desk were the remains of an appeal someone had been preparing for the mail, letters and contribution envelopes in neat piles.

Nikki took out her notebook. "I'm going to have to ask you about Mr. Zaporelli."

Karen's face seemed to droop at the mention of his name. She lifted her hair behind her ears again—it had slipped out when she'd sipped at the drink. Nikki suspected the hair-lifting was a nervous gesture, something Karen did when she was trying to collect herself. She flicked her hand to give consent, but Nikki caught a subtle change in her chin line, as though she were chewing the inside of her lip.

"You were Mr. Zaporelli's campaign manager?"

She seemed not to have heard. Her glance was clouded, unhappy. Nikki said gently, "You worked for Mr. Zaporelli?"

She roused herself. "I was in charge of the office, yes."

"What exactly did you do?"

"I—" Strong emotion caught her unaware. "What good is all this? He's dead, isn't he? Whoever did this is out there, running around free while you—" She opened a drawer and slammed it shut so hard the Worcestershire sauce fell over, dripping on the wood. She stared at the spill a full moment, then said, her voice breaking, "I—I'm sorry." She reached into a black suede pouch on the floor, pressed a handkerchief to her eyes, blew her nose.

"Who do *you* think killed him?" Nikki asked.

"Some nut. The city's full of them. He wanted to be in Albany—serve the people. God help him!" Fresh tears surfaced. She blotted her eyes, took another sip from the cup.

Nikki waited till she was more composed, then said, "The garage manager told me he was alone yesterday when he took the car." Karen balled the handkerchief tightly in her fist. "You usually met him on Tuesday, didn't you?"

"Yes. I'd go to his mother's with him, out in Brooklyn."

"But you didn't yesterday."

"No." She moved her head so that her hair fell forward, hid her eyes. "I went home. I was beginning to feel sick then— whatever's bothering me had started to come on." She held the handkerchief over her eyes again, then pulled it away. Her mouth turned down at the corners. "I blame myself for what happened. I should have gone with him no matter how I felt. He made that trip dozens of times when I was along and nothing ever— The one time I stayed home—" Her voice doubled back on her as though she were choking on her guilt.

"He went to see his mother every Tuesday?"

"That's right."

"You went, too?"

"Well, I didn't go in—" She lifted a tissue from the drawer, let it soak up the puddle of Worcestershire sauce. "I waited in the car."

"How come?"

"Well—He was married, you know. And his mother was an old lady. He didn't want to upset her, have her think things—"

"Were there things to think?"

Karen hesitated, twisting the handkerchief into a long spiral. "I might as well tell you before you hear it from anyone else—we were lovers, Dean and I."

"So you just went along for the ride."

"Yes. It gave us a chance to talk, catch up."

"How long would he stay inside, with his mother?"

"An hour, the most. I'd bring a book or read the paper. When he came out, we'd have dinner and we ... He'd take me home."

"Where do you live?"

"Two blocks from here. Fifty-sixth and Second."

"When did you get to your apartment yesterday?"

"Let's see—Maybe three thirty, four."

"And you stayed there?"

"I told you—I wasn't feeling well."

Nikki made some notes, watched Karen out of the corner of her eye. "You manage the office?"

"Yes, the volunteers, the supplies, and all that."

"How long have you been working for him?"

"Four years. He—" Any mention of him seemed to freshen the flow of tears. "We were planning to get married."

"When?"

"When his divorce was final."

"When would that have been?"

She hesitated. "After the election—"

"He'd actually been to a lawyer?"

She dropped the handkerchief on the desk, letting it unwind slowly. "Of course."

"You had a definite date?"

"Next spring. He wanted to avoid a public fuss right now."

Nikki thought of Donna Zaporelli's words: "He said it was bad for his image."

"Did his wife know?"

She lifted the cup, sipped. "I don't know what she knew." She stared into the cup. When she looked up, her eyes were full again. "It's hard to believe he's dead."

Her gaze turned inward, searching for the dream that was no longer there. Nikki had once been on a case where a husband had killed his wife; she'd seen the same expression of grief. He'd strangled her in a moment of rage. When it was over, he was filled with genuine remorse, a sense of loss.

"I'm sorry," Nikki said.

Karen swallowed, the sound audible. "I want to know who did this to him," she said. "I want to see the monster with my own eyes."

# 7

She circled the station house once, telling herself she was looking for a parking spot, noticing all the while that Dave's car was nowhere in sight. Had she expected him to be here? She wasn't sure but was aware she was disappointed when she couldn't find him.

She raced up to the Detective Squad and heard shouts behind Eagle-Eye's door: Borough Chief Dritzer saying something about a "goddamn prima donna lady detective," Eagle-Eye soothing him. The door opened a crack and she could hear more clearly. Dritzer said, ". . . pressure on every fucking level, all the way down the line. I'm talking about the mayor—" Eagle-Eye's response was too low to hear.

Dritzer came out. He was a balding, chunky little man, a hero-type who held himself stiffly erect, military-style. He was the one who'd left the print on top of the murder car this morning. He gave Nikki a cold blue stare, then turned and pummeled down the steps.

She entered the office, sidled past Stavich, and took a seat opposite the long triangular piece of wood on Eagle-Eye's desk that said "John J. Parcowicz, Squad Commander" in gilt letters. "What's eating Dritzer?" she said.

Eagle-Eye said sweetly, "Welcome home, Detective Trakos," then, "Where the hell ya been?" She could always guess the amount of stress he was feeling by how close together his eyes looked. On bad days they seemed to migrate toward one another. Today they were only millimeters apart. "Missed the whole damn conference. How many times I have to tell you—you got a lead, we wanna know about it. This ain't the movies—"

"It's real life," she finished for him.

"Very funny."

In the year she'd been on the squad she'd closed five cases, built good cases that would play in court. Sometime over that year she'd learned she could needle Eagle-Eye, as some of the other detectives did. As long as she didn't push him too far. "What is it with Dritzer?"

He leaned forward. "He wants you out. Too big a case—he wants a heavy hitter."

She felt a spike of anger. She'd been hoping against hope this wouldn't happen, that the big brass would let her keep the case. Well, she wasn't going to give it up without a fight.

She opened her mouth to defend herself, but Eagle-Eye waved his hand in her face. "I talked myself around the block, Trakos—bought you a coupla days. I don't know how long he'll stay convinced. Read me?"

"I read you."

Stavich took out his Camels but Eagle-Eye said, "Not in here. I got this sinus thing—the smoke drives me nuts." He rubbed the bridge of his nose, looked at Nikki again. "Will it be all right if I summarize, Trakos, since you weren't able to attend our little meeting today?"

"I'd appreciate it, sir." She rarely called him *sir* anymore, saw his quick reaction as he looked up to let her know he'd caught the mockery in her tone.

"Zap was on his way to visit his mother," he said. "According to the mother, sister, and a couple of aunts who live with them, he never made it."

Stavich said, "But he musta been done somewhere near the crime scene. Otherwise, if he was done in Manhattan say, the perp's riding around with a stiff in the car."

"If he was shot in Manhattan," Nikki said, "and the killer dropped him in Brooklyn, how'd the killer get home?"

"That's what I mean—the perp did him in Brooklyn."

"He'd still have to figure out how to get out of there once he dumped the body."

Stavich said, "Unless he lived close."

"What about the subway?"

"Nah, it's nowhere near there."

"What'd the house canvass show?" she asked.

"Zero."

"No one heard the shot?"

"No."

"And the auto canvass?"

"Same."

Eagle-Eye cut in. "Boys and girls, can I have your attention? Stavich was nice enough to tell me, Trakos, that you saw the wife and that he put in a call to her doctor to find out how sick she is. What about the son? Dritzer's real hot on the son, thinks that's where we ought to focus."

Nikki said, "Stavich went to Bellevue, where the roommate works—"

"He hasn't been there in two days," Stavich said. "I got his home address."

Nikki said, "We'll check his place tonight."

Eagle-Eye nodded. "If it isn't too much trouble."

"Zap's wife claims the son was nowhere near the apartment yesterday," she said, "but the garage attendant puts him there the same time as Zap."

"Thank you for that interesting little bit, Trakos. As your squad commander, I'm grateful for every crumb you can share with us." He ran his finger down the legal pad before him. "Jameson's checking into the cook and the maid, but it doesn't look like that'll take us anywhere." He ticked off more assignments, listed reports still outstanding from the Medical Examiner, Ballistics, the Latent Print Department.

From outside the door she heard Dave's voice. She was warmed by the sound. She told herself she wanted to run the case by him, get his reactions. That was why she wanted to see him.

"That's it," Eagle-Eye said. He concentrated his nearsighted gaze on Nikki. "Detective Trakos, Chief Dritzer and I and a few of the guys're planning another get-together tomorrow at the same time. We'd like to invite you—that is, if you're not too busy working the case on your own?" He leaned forward. His right eye seemed about to leap the narrow bridge of his nose to join the left one. "One other thing." He lifted a folded newspaper at the side of his desk, slapped it down in front of Nikki. "Are you responsible for this piece a shit?" She glanced down, saw her picture in the paper, the chain-link fence of the marina behind her, and read the headline: COPS BAFFLED ON ZAP KILLING. She hadn't said that! Or had she? She couldn't remember her exact words.

"In case you're confused, *I* talk to the newspapers," Eagle-Eye said. "You do the detecting. Got it?"

"Got it." She glanced at the first paragraph. "Detectives assigned to the murder of Dean Zaporelli admitted this morning they had no promising leads. Because of Mr. Zaporelli's prominence, the sluggishness of this investigation serves to highlight the general bureaucratic morass in which the police department operates, its lack of imagination, its—" She thought of the reporter with the Orphan Annie haircut and felt her fingers itch with an urge to strangle her.

She said, "That's not what I—"

"*I* handle info to the press. Me or the DCPI." The Deputy Commissioner of Public Information. "Okay?"

"Okay."

He rose to indicate the conference was over. Stavich opened the door for her. She was about to leave when Eagle-Eye called, "Trakos—"

"Yes?"

"Watch your step on this one. Careers are at stake—mostly yours."

# 8

Dave was nowhere in sight when she stepped into the squad room. She could have sworn she'd heard him. Suddenly it seemed late. She felt herself droop, felt exhausted.

Stavich said, "I'm going to the john. Meet you at the car." They would head back to Manhattan and look for Matt Zaporelli.

She ordered a Bureau of Criminal Investigation check on Karen Royce. She sensed Karen was holding back information. To protect Zaporelli or herself? The BCI check would turn up a jail record, if there was one. Karen didn't seem the type to have spent time in jail, but you never knew.

A pile of white slips lay in Nikki's message slot, calls on pending cases. But she'd been taken "off the chart"—her cases would wait until she'd cleared Zaporelli's killing. Or had been relieved of the investigation.

What if she *couldn't* find the killer? They seemed to be dealing with a well-organized murderer who was neat at the crime scene and left few clues. That kind was hard to trace. What if they couldn't catch him? The case would be shoved into an "open" file—unsolved homicides were never closed. Something in her rebelled at the idea. She thought of the shooter gunning Zaporelli down, coolly delivering a second bullet between his legs after he'd died. She'd find him. She wouldn't rest till she did. She would be just as merciless in her hunt as the killer had been in the murder.

There was no message from Dave. She realized she'd been expecting to find one. She walked down the steps. Had she really heard his voice? Or had she been wishing so hard she'd tricked her ears? She felt empty and confused, as she did whenever they had a fight. Somehow it was worse this time; she had the feeling of finality, of closure.

Outside, a couple blocked her path. Both were robust and broad-shouldered; they wore leather coats, the man's shorter, showing his jeans, the woman's fur-collared. The woman wore heavy eye makeup, runny from recent tears.

"Plizz, lady," the man said to Nikki. "Not spikk Englizz." He pointed to the woman. "Still pocket. Take money."

The woman nodded vehemently. Fresh tears squeezed out of the corners of her eyes.

"She was robbed?"

"*Da*. Robbed," the man repeated.

"You speak Russian?"

His eyes lit with hope. "*Da, da.*" The precinct bordered Little Odessa, a community of Russian immigrants in Brighton Beach.

"Go inside and tell them you speak Russian." Cook and Bernardi had taken a crash course in the language and would be able to interpret for them.

"Very much thanks," the man said.

Gusts of wind whipped the bushes on the strip of green along the front of the station house. It had turned colder. This morning the forecasters had promised the high would be fifty. They had apologized later. It was late March, but real spring weather seemed months away. She tugged her jacket down, wished she'd taken her coat. It would be a long, cold night, hours before she'd be home.

She thought of her niece, Lara. Would Lara remember where the extra blanket was and take it from the closet if it was cold? What was she doing tonight, anyhow? Nikki remembered suddenly that she'd promised to help Lara with a project for tomorrow's science fair—a comparison of recoil in the five main types of handguns. Lara had given up her early interest in boats and was fascinated by guns, finger-prints, forensic detail. Nikki was troubled by this new obses-sion. Dave had tried to reassure her—with a cop as a parent it was normal for Lara to be interested in crime. She'd been listening to Nikki for five years, ever since Nikki had taken her in. His kids had gone through a similar phase; Dave was a widower with a grown son and daughter. Lara, he pointed out, was interested in other things, too. Cooking, for instance, reading, and gymnastics.

He'd helped Lara set up the chart for the project, suggest-ed which guns to illustrate. What needed to be done tonight was the math. No way Mrs. Binsey, the world's most unin-volved sitter, would be willing or able to help. Lara, an uncertain math student at best, would have to hand the pro-ject in late. Another dollop of guilt for Nikki to swallow.

The plainclothes cars were parked around the side of the station house. Nikki turned the corner, saw Dave leaning against the Fury, and felt a thump under her heart. The glow of the street lamp shadowed his eyes, bronzed his cheeks. His skin was ruddy but fine, darker at the jaw. She remembered the feel of his jaw against her cheeks, how her own skin red-dened after hours of lovemaking. Her face grew warm with the memory.

"I heard you upstairs," she said. He leaned back to study her, his eyes narrowed. She waited uncertainly, put off by his silence. "I have to go back to the city."

"Zaporelli?"

"Yes. Look, maybe we can get together sometime, talk about the case." She tried to meet his glance but he looked past her at the curb. She followed his glance, watched the flow of traffic on Coney Island Avenue, saw a lone pedestri-an, a Hasidic man with a tall black hat and long sideburns, hands dug into his pockets, hurrying along, the wind pushing him. His hat blew off, exposing the yarmulke, or skullcap, he wore underneath. He chased the hat a few feet, brushed it off, and clamped it back on his head.

"I can't figure you out," Dave said. "I ask you to marry me and it's like I'm giving you a death sentence."

"It isn't you—I love you."

He looked at her directly for the first time. "Then what's the problem?"

"Marriage itself."

"You never want to get married?"

"I'm not sure. I'm *already* married, to the job—"

"I know all that—I'm a cop, too."

But he *didn't* know. A man was *expected* to be married to his job. A woman . . . "Your wife didn't work outside of the house." Dave had lost his wife ten years before.

"So?" he said.

"I don't know if I can do *this*"—she inclined her head toward the station house—"and be a wife too. I broke up with a guy once because he couldn't share me with the job." It had been during her academy training. She and Mark had been teenage sweethearts, had been planning to announce their engagement. "He couldn't take the crazy hours, and he hated it that I worked with other guys all day."

He touched her cheek, brushed a strand of hair off her face. "He wasn't a cop, that's the difference."

"But you'd expect—"

"Give it a shot, Nikki. Let me—"

His glance was caught by something behind her. She turned and saw Stavich coming toward them. "I have to go," she said.

Dave walked away, his jaw tight.

# 9

Glenn Taylor and Matt Zaporelli shared a loft at 522 Spring Street in SoHo, an area of the city that had been industrial years ago and was now a conglomeration of art studios and galleries. Five twenty-two was a brick building whose iron staircase had been painted violet. At ground level a gallery showed brass and marble sculpture.

Nikki and Stavich climbed the staircase to the entry, feet clanging on the metal. It wasn't as windy in Manhattan, but it had turned colder, the air crisp and biting. Nikki pressed the button marked "Taylor" on the security board.

"Zaporelli's kid ain't listed," Stavich remarked as they waited.

"Maybe he doesn't want anyone to know where he lives. His mother, for instance." She pushed the buzzer again.

A window opened above their heads. "Yes?" a woman called. She leaned from a fourth-story window, young, fresh-faced in spite of the late hour, dark hair swinging forward, streaks of it dyed alternately green and cranberry. "You buzz?"

"Is Matt Zaporelli home?"

"Nope."

"Glenn Taylor?"

"Neither one."

"Can we come up and talk to you?"

She hesitated, and Nikki added, "We're the police."

"The fuzz?" She smiled. "Sure, come on. Fourth floor."

Stavich mumbled, "A buncha characters—that's what you got in this city." They entered the hallway, headed up the wooden steps. The walls were graffitied with pictures of a female figure on a cross, two men performing fellatio, a herd of sheep with human torsos. Stavich panted harder with each step, rested on the landings. "Too old for this shit."

By the time they reached the fourth floor the young woman had opened her door and was standing in front of it. "My cousin's a cop, in Queens." She held out her hand. "Meredith Compton. I sublet here."

It was hard to focus on her face without being drawn to the two-toned hair. Nikki asked, "You sublet from—"

"Glenn, Glenn Taylor. It isn't really legal. The landlord doesn't know." She was under twenty, pretty, with a quick, responsive face and a tendency toward plumpness. She wore a silver nose ring, shorts under a paint-stained shirt sizes too large, nothing on her feet. A feather bracelet that looked Native American circled one ankle.

Nikki asked, "Matt lives here?"

"Matty? Sure. He's Glenn's roommate—lover, actually. Come on in."

She trotted ahead of them through the hallway, happy to have company even though it was pushing ten. A bell on the feather anklet made a tiny jingling sound when she moved. "These are my paintings." She gestured toward the wall. Nikki got a quick impression of mud, discolored wood, and mushrooms. "Nice," she murmured. The lines around Stavich's mouth deepened.

"People have really been encouraging."

They entered an open living area. For an instant Nikki thought she was at a photo exhibit featuring Matt Zaporelli. Almost a whole wall was devoted to him. She recognized the picture she'd seen on his mother's nightstand, enlarged to poster size. Nearby was an actual poster—for an appearance at the Blue Boy Cafe, West Street. Nikki recognized the name of the place the garage attendant had mentioned, the gay club where he'd gone to hear Matt sing. The other photos were smaller—Matt leaning against a tree, Matt striding down a city street, Matt in costume at a Halloween parade. A nude study, almost a silhouette, showed him on a bed. Nikki was struck again by the beauty of his face, the almost sculpted features, fine, expressive eyes. One picture she found particularly interesting looked unposed. Matt stood on the beach, faced out toward the water. He seemed wide-eyed, frightened, his usual rebellious look replaced by uncertainty.

Plants clustered at each of the six tall windows spaced evenly along the wall. Hung from the ceiling and on swing bars attached to the sash, they crowded the sills and the floor. The greenery softened the bare, curtainless windows.

Meredith caught Nikki looking at the plants and said, "That's Glenn's jungle. He's a plant freak."

Stavich cast around for a place to sit. The room was neat and well-organized but sparsely furnished. Books lined the baseboards, set up on makeshift shelves separated by bricks. Deeper inside the loft was a sofa and love-seat arrangement, two tired pieces covered with sheets, set around a low table. Stavich pointed to a wooden chair within reach and said, "Mind if I—?"

Meredith sprang forward, positioned the chair, and offered to get Nikki one, too.

Nikki shook her head. "Do you know where Matt is?"

"That's the thing—*no one* seems to. Glenn's frantic, hasn't seen or heard from him since yesterday. He's out looking for him now. He's been back a bunch of times today to see if he showed up."

Nikki pointed toward the wall.

"Who took all the pictures?"

"Glenn. He freelances in his spare time, does pretty well."

"Those are all pictures of Matt, aren't they?"

"That's right. He's going to be a singer. Some of those are publicity shots."

"He get a lot of work?"

"Not really. He did a gig this fall at the Blue Boy, but it only lasted a few nights. He hasn't done much since."

Nikki looked across the shining oak floor, past the sofa and love seat. At the far end of the loft copper pots hung over the window; a table and chairs nestled nearby. "It sounds like Matt's not able to help much with the rent."

"Glenn doesn't care. He'd go buy the moon for Matty if that's what he wanted. He pays for his singing coach and voice lessons."

"His parents don't pay for that stuff?"

"Oh no. His mom would like to, but she doesn't have that kind of money."

Nikki remembered the luxurious furnishings in Zaporelli's apartment, Donna's fashionable robe. She wondered whether Donna *couldn't* pay for her son's training or chose not to.

"Glenn would do more," Meredith said, "but Matty won't let him. Too proud. Once in a while Matty gets himself into a real funk—he's shit, Glenn's doing too much, he doesn't want to take anything from him—you know. Then Glenn calms him down and it's over." She looked toward the kitchen area. "Coffee?"

"No, thanks," Nikki said. "Would you say Matt was that way recently—that he didn't want Glenn to support him?"

The girl thought for a moment, then nodded. "He carried on a lot."

"Okay if I smoke?" Stavich asked.

"Sure." Meredith ran into the hall, jingling as she went, came back with an ashtray. "This is about Matty's father, isn't it. I'll tell you whatever I can if it'll help. My cousin was explaining how hard it is to be a cop in this city. I mean, anything I can do—"

"Appreciate that," Nikki said.

"I do know Matty didn't get along with his father. The problem was money. Matty said his dad had cheated him out of thousands of dollars. Every now and then when Matty decided he was being a parasite, that it wasn't fair to Glenn, he'd go uptown to try to get money from his folks. Forget it—a lost cause. His father didn't want him to go into singing. He thought if he cut off his money, he'd give it up."

"You said 'his money.' Matt had an allowance?"

"I'm not sure. He never really explained it—"

She stopped abruptly as the door slammed. A man called, "Meredith?" on a note of rising anxiety.

"In here."

"Did he phone? Did you hear anything—"

He turned into the living area, a thin, tired man in his forties, wearing dark-rimmed glasses that magnified the worry in his eyes. "Who're you?" he asked Nikki and Stavich.

"Police." Nikki showed her badge. "We're looking for Matt Zaporelli."

His eyes blinked behind the glasses, but not quickly enough to hide the fear. "He's not here. I'm his roommate, Glenn Taylor." His glance darted to Meredith, a line forming between his brows. "How long have they been here?" he asked.

"A few minutes, I guess."

"What did you tell them?"

Meredith seemed flustered. "Nothing, really. I mean—"

He glared at her, and she fell into silence.

"Where is Matt, Mr. Taylor?" Nikki asked.

"I have no idea. I wish I did." He pulled the tab of his jacket zipper down, then slid it back up. She'd expected him to be younger, probably because both Matt and Meredith were, but he was the papa of the arrangement, at least twenty years their senior. He was dressed in a black leather jacket, worn jeans, brand-name tennis shoes that had once been white. His dark hair was thinning, showing specks of gray.

"Can we sit down?" he said. Exhaustion tugged at his face, but his eyes were wary, restless and unsettled. He led them toward the seating arrangement, flopped into a corner of the sofa, and gestured toward the chairs.

Nikki asked, "When's the last time you saw Matt?"

He unzipped the jacket partway, gripped the tab tightly as though he were holding onto his sanity, afraid he'd lose it if he let go. "Last night, at about eight o'clock. We were shopping at this mall in Jersey—near Fort Lee. We both needed clothes, so I didn't go to work—I'm an orderly at Bellevue."

Meredith fingered the bell on her anklet as he spoke. She glanced up as though she wanted to interrupt but Glenn intercepted her, said, "Meredith, you don't have to sit through this. We'll call if we need you." She slid off the chair reluctantly and walked into the hallway. Her bell made a sad sound as she left.

Nikki said to Glenn, "You were saying you spent the day with Matt."

"We left here at noon, stayed in Jersey till after eight. We had dinner at the mall, then Matty said he wanted to go to a movie I'd already seen, so I left him there and went home."

"How come you were out looking for him just now—didn't he get back last night?" Nikki remembered what Meredith had said, that Matt hadn't been home since yesterday.

He swallowed, his Adam's apple a sharp pebble in his throat. "He did—but this morning when the news came on about his father he was terribly upset—I couldn't calm him. We sat right here, and I kept talking to him. Then I left him for a minute—just a single minute—and when I got back he was gone." He'd recited this story in a flat, unengaged tone. Now his face changed and genuine terror came into it. "I don't like the way he looked—he wasn't himself. I went out looking for him, but no one's seen him. He just disappeared."

"It's funny," Nikki said, "a garage attendant in Mr.

Zaporelli's building says he saw Matt *there* about five thirty yesterday afternoon. A man named Tom MacFadden."

"He's lying!" He blanched. "I tell you we were together all day and we were—"

"Mr. Taylor, you and I both want the same thing, to help Matt—"

"Don't fuck with me, lady." His lips tightened, the words squeezing out between them like hard little pellets. "The cops don't want to help anyone but themselves. You'll stick him with his father's murder if you can. He didn't do shit!"

As a rule she didn't tolerate gutter language. It showed disrespect for the police. She felt Stavich stiffen beside her and weighed her options—she could come down hard, act like Jane Wayne or Dirty Harriet, let Taylor know who was boss. Or she could ignore his outburst. She might learn more from this frightened man without a show of strength. "Mr. Taylor, the doorman and garage manager said they saw him come in. Why would all of them lie?"

His eyes had the look of a drowning man's—panic, rage, the loss of hope that some miracle would save him.

She said, "We can search for him better than you can—"

"You'll hunt him down like a dog! He's not some dumb cluck— He's sensitive. To the point where he might—" His voice cracked. "I met him at Bellevue. They brought him in eight months ago, an OD—"

"A druggie?"

"No. He took all the pills he could lay his hands on— aspirin, sleeping pills, you name it. He wanted to check out."

"Why?"

His glance darted sideways. "He wouldn't say. We pumped him clean and he lived. He wasn't happy, I'll tell you. But I took care of him, gave him a new start. I'm *still* taking care of him. You want to louse all that up?"

She held his glance, stared him down.

A long minute passed. Glenn said, "We went to his folks yesterday." His mouth pinched, slackened. He looked past Nikki at the wall of photos and swallowed hard. Stavich lit a fresh cigarette from the stub of the old one, crushed the butt in the ashtray. Nikki waited. "I took a personal day so I could go with him. He'd been upset. He got that way."

"About anything special?"

The zipper tab moved down half an inch. "That he wasn't contributing anything here, that his father wouldn't talk to him about . . . anything."

Why had he hesitated? There was another pause as he seemed to lose his train of thought, then collect himself. "He wouldn't let me go up with him, said I was being too protective. I waited in front of Bloomie's, told him I'd meet him there."

"What time was that?"

"When he left me? Three, three thirty. I didn't see him again till close to six." His eyes widened as he remembered. "He came back like a wild man! His face was bruised, he had this big lump on his jaw." His hands came to his sides, fists clenching. "His father socked him! He'd— The man was an animal! He *deserved* to die! I don't care what happened to him—he had it coming!"

"Did he tell you *why* his father hit him?"

"He was too crazy—he couldn't. He tried to get away from me. I was holding his arm but somehow he pulled free, took off and ran. I chased him around Bloomie's, down Lex, and I lost him. Around Lex and Fifty-first. I ran around in circles for a while. Then I came back here. I figured he had to come home sooner or later."

"But he didn't."

"No. I don't know where he is."

"You were looking for him at about seven last night?"

"I was here, waiting. I thought he'd show up."

"Anyone see you here?"

"No. I was alone. Meredith works part-time. Wait a minute—is that when his old man got it? Listen, I didn't kill the bastard. I wish I had, but someone saved me the trouble. I was waiting for Matty to call. I sat around till ten or so, then hit some local places, the bars, movies, restaurants. No one's seen him." The tab slid up, down again over the same inch of track. "He has no money."

"Maybe he went to his mother's to get some."

His mouth twisted to the side. "*She* doesn't have any. Zaporelli held every nickel. He used to let her charge things, but never gave her hard cash. He knew she'd give it to Matt." Mentioning Matt's name seemed to return him to the core of his worry. "Where can you be in this city without a cent? Where could he have slept?" He looked at Nikki as if she knew, his eyes begging her to tell him.

The phone rang in the hallway and he sprang up. Stavich rose and stretched, frowned at a muddy canvas that looked like more of Meredith's work. Nikki glanced idly at a magazine that lay open on the coffee table, skimmed it quickly. It was about the Lantern Light Playhouse, an off-Broadway theater that seemed to be jinxed. A young girl connected with it had died of an overdose thirteen years ago. A photo showed the pile of trash bags where her body had been found.

From the hallway Nikki heard Glenn's voice. "Where exactly?" He sounded excited.

Nikki scanned the article again, glanced at a paragraph that recalled something familiar. Bernard Chase, the theater's founder, had been shot in a hotel room six years ago. The Nose-Job murder, detectives had called it—why? She couldn't remember.

She heard Glenn say, "Thanks for calling." An instant later he stood in the doorway and saw her holding the magazine. He came across the room and snatched it from her. "*That's* where it is! I was looking for it." He shoved it into his jacket. "Can we wrap this up? I want to go out again."

Stavich said, breaking in, "If we had a picture of your buddy Matt, it would help."

Glenn reached into a drawer and handed them a recent four-by-five shot. He saw them to the door.

Outside on the hallway staircase Stavich signaled her to linger. They walked slowly down to the next landing and stood near the mural of the two men coupling. Stavich lit a cigarette, let a minute go by. Nikki was about to urge him down the steps when they heard Glenn shout from above. "Can't you ever keep your mouth shut?" A beat of silence. Nikki's stomach knotted. Blows sometimes accompanied anger that intense. But all she heard was more shouting. "That's my business. Mine and Matty's. If I want to tell them, I'll tell them."

Silence, then the door above them opened. Stavich motioned her downstairs quickly. They reached ground level and hid under the violet staircase. Glenn Taylor came tearing out of the building, hands dug into his pockets, shoulders hunched.

Stavich threw his cigarette toward the gutter. "I'm goin' after him." A thin trail of vapor steamed from his mouth.

"I'll get the car—"

"No, better I'm alone."

She started to protest but he shook his head. "He'd make the two of us in a second."

She knew he was right, that Glenn could easily spot her and Stavich if he suspected he was being followed; a lone man was less visible. Yet she hated letting him go off alone. The streets weren't safe at this hour. She thought of all the things that might happen to him.

He was surprisingly quick for a large man. Glenn turned

the corner but Stavich was only a few yards behind. An instant later he was out of sight.

She waited to make sure Glenn wasn't coming back. Then she turned, ran up the violet steps again, and pressed the buzzer.

# 10

"Glenn doesn't want me to talk to you," Meredith said.

They stood in the doorway of the loft. The girl's eyes were red-rimmed, her voice husky.

"You want to help," Nikki said. "Don't you?"

Meredith bit her lip. With her punk-dyed hair she looked like a sad clown. "I was wrong to let you come in before, to talk to you. Glenn's been good to me. He lets me have my space rent-free pretty much. I mean, I owe him."

"But if you know something that could give us a lead— Look, whoever killed Matt's father could kill again. That's a pretty heavy thing when you think about it."

Meredith sucked in more of her lip, chewed on it. "I'm not even sure if what I know would help you." Nikki was about to urge her to tell it anyhow, let Nikki decide how valuable it was when Meredith said, "You'd better go. Glenn might come back any minute."

Nikki tugged the strap of her purse higher on her shoulder. The girl knew something, had a piece that might connect. She wasn't going to leave without it, not if she had to shake it out of her.

She had a sudden inspiration. "Okay. If that's how you feel." She moved toward the steps, then stopped as though she'd just remembered something. "What precinct did you say your cousin was in? If I run across him, I'll say hello."

"He's a rookie, in Forest Hills," the girl answered. "His

name's Compton, like mine. Jim Compton." Something changed behind her glance. "Look, it's not that I don't care—I'm in a tough position."

"I understand." Nikki held her glance, waited.

"What the hell!" Meredith said. "There isn't much I know. It's just—Glenn lied to you. Matty didn't go up to his folks to ask why his father wasn't talking to him. He found something that was going to turn everything around, he told Glenn. He wanted to confront his father with it. Glenn told him to leave it alone, it would get Matty into trouble, wouldn't get him what he wanted anyhow."

"What was it he found?"

"I don't know. Look, that's all I have—you'd better go. And if you talk to Glenn, please leave me out of this. I never told you anything."

# 11

Nikki jackknifed her long legs into her Camaro and drove up Coney Island Avenue toward home. Someday, if she no longer wanted to be a cop, she and the Camaro could qualify as a circus act. "Watch the giant woman as she folds herself into the tiny car!" A moment of impulse—she'd fallen in love with the car's sporty look. She'd had to live with four years of discomfort afterward. She'd forgotten to take into account the length of her legs, hadn't realized that getting in and out of the car would be such a challenge. If she had it to do all over again, would she make the same choice?

She was weary as she pulled off Foster Avenue onto her street. One A.M. Lawn and porch lights glowed, guarding the peaceful houses. Families slept behind the broad lawns, in the comfortable century-old homes under the sycamores. Only she was still awake, prowling the night like a hungry wolf.

She slowed along the oval dividers with their cobbled edge and stopped at the roomy brown Victorian that housed her apartment. A row of graceful lilac and forsythia shrubs banked the house, their branches still winter-bare, tossed by the wind. Snowdrops, the earliest bulbs, poked up underneath, their brave white heads dancing in the cold. She waited for her stress level to drop—usually the sight of the old house and garden took the edge off the day's tension. Tonight, for some reason, that didn't happen.

She glanced up above the billowing porch to Lara's bed-

room. It was dark. At least her niece was asleep. A dim blue
light flickered from the living-room window. Mrs. Binsey
watched TV or slept on the sofa while the idiot box played, the
baby-sitter with her electronic baby-sitter. She shouldn't be so
critical of Mrs. Binsey. At least the woman was willing to be
here at all kinds of hours—what would she do without her?

She backed into the drive, scanning the area with "street
eyes." She'd developed a special way of looking at a street as a
patrol officer ten years ago, a way of spotting someone out of
place or engaged in a suspicious activity. She'd once prevent-
ed a crime, only blocks away. A disheveled-looking man had
been following a young woman on her way home from the subway. The man looked unkempt, his clothing torn and dirty, a
misfit in this otherwise respectable neighborhood. Nikki, driving home from a tour of duty, had seen the man edge closer
and closer to the woman. She'd stopped the car as he'd
reached into his victim's purse. Nikki had jumped from the
car, gun out, and identified herself as a police officer, had held
the man until backup came.

Now, as she swept her glance around the quiet street a car
started half a block away at the corner of De Koven Court, a
Chevy Caprice. She sat up straighter and watched it approach,
knowing it was Dave. She wanted to be with him; it seemed so
natural to end the day that way. But wouldn't that encourage
him to think they had a future together? She didn't want to
give him hope if she wasn't sure, and right now she felt only
confusion.

He came to the passenger side of the car, tapped on the
window. "Let me in," he said. "It's cold out here." She released the door locks and he slid in next to her. "Where you
been?" he asked.

"Looking for Zaporelli's son."

"Any luck?"

"No. Stavich tailed the roommate, lost him somewhere

around Forty-second Street. The roommate claims he doesn't know where Zaporelli's son is. He's looking for him too."

"You believe him?"

She thought for a moment, remembered Glenn's frantic face, the panic in his voice. "Yes."

"I put out a bulletin on Zaporelli's kid," she said, "but I don't feel right. I should be out there looking for him."

"Hey—you're human."

"Stavich is sleeping at the station—I just came from there." She'd felt frustrated that she'd had to leave, had wished for a moment she didn't have Lara at home and could devote herself entirely to her work the way some of the other detectives did. At times whatever she did on a case wasn't enough.

"You're not missing anything," Dave said. "You'll be back at work before most of those characters wake up."

His reassurance made her want to cry. He could be the most supportive person in the world—her best friend. She felt a mix of emotions—she needed to be apart from him so she could think about their future, but there was comfort in his presence, in discussing the case with him.

She tipped her head closer, and he kissed her, his lips evoking memories of past pleasure, arousing her.

"Come back to my place," he said gruffly.

She had an impulse to go, fought it. "Not till I know what I want to do."

He pulled away, leaned against the window, watched a trickle of moisture run down the windshield. The trickle grew into a full-sized drop and rolled toward the wipers. "I don't know if I can do this, hang around while you make up your mind."

She suddenly felt impatient. She'd lived through the longest day of her life, had eaten a soggy frankfurter for dinner, skipped lunch altogether. Why was he pressing her for an answer *now*? "Why can't we go on the way we were?"

"Because we can't!"

"Marriage isn't the only way two people can be committed to each other, you know."

"It is for me. I don't like living this way. We don't have a place we can call our own. You get out of my bed in the middle of the night and run home. We grab an hour here, an hour there. It's no good. I want to make a life with you."

"You're old-fashioned—"

"Maybe. But that's *me.*" He reached for the handle. The door's slam echoed through the quiet street.

She wanted to tell him that things changed once a woman married, that a few minutes in front of a minister could ruin a relationship, burdening it with expectancy and resentment. If they married it would be okay for her to work, have a little job somewhere, but a profession? He was back inside the Chevy now, pulling onto Foster, moving quickly out of sight.

She dragged herself up the porch and then up the stairs to her apartment. Mrs. Binsey slept on the sofa while Claudette Colbert and Clark Gable hitched a ride on a country road. She woke Mrs. Binsey up and sent her home, grateful for the peace of the apartment. Why was Dave always adding complication to her life? Why couldn't he leave well enough alone? They could have gone on for years the way they were.

She shuffled down the hall to look in on Lara. Her niece lay sprawled in sleep, blond hair spread like silk over the pillow. Nikki was about to shut the door when she caught sight of the science fair project, a white oak-tag chart. Five guns had been silhouetted on the left, their recoils noted on the right. She overcame the revulsion that ran through her every time she saw the chart—should a ten-year-old be studying forensics?—and noticed that Lara had completed the project. The penciled numbers had been inked in green ballpoint. Had Lara decided to take a chance that the math was right? A tiny note lay under the chart, a slip of paper from Lara's memo pad. "Dear Mom— Uncle Dave helped me with the math. XXX, Lara."

Was the note more propaganda on Lara's part—her way of

letting Nikki know Dave was an essential part of their lives? The next moment she felt ashamed of her resentment, overcome by compassion for Lara, grateful for Dave's closeness to the girl. Lara had been transformed over the past year. Once a lonely gnome, she'd stopped hiding from the neighborhood kids. She was doing well in school. She even had a best friend.

An ache came over her, regret for the way she and Dave had parted tonight. What he wanted—a full and permanent commitment from her—wasn't a bad thing in itself. But was it right for *her*?

She'd worked hard to get where she was. Months in the academy studying marksmanship, regs, strategy, toughening her body, stretching her brain. Then three years on patrol, walking through the Bedford-Stuyvesant ghetto, finding out her six-foot height and white skin made her a big target for black anger, learning how to take care of herself. Then Public Morals, a losing battle against gambling, hundreds of raids on illegal operations run in shabby bodegas on the Lower East Side, where the immigrant owners struggled to survive. And finally, last year, promotion to detective. She was convinced she'd come this far because she'd been traveling fairly light. She'd had Lara, true, but she hadn't had to divide herself between the job and marriage.

She sat in the kitchen and read a letter from her mother addressed to both Nikki and Lara. Nikki called her parents in Florida every weekend; clinging to frugal immigrant habits, her mother answered with a weekly letter. She wrote that she'd attended cousin Irini's wedding, an impressive affair. "Irini wore a beautiful dress. She is about your size, only a little shorter. I told her take good care of the gown. You would not be ashamed to be married in such a dress, Nikki."

Nikki let the sheet flutter to the table. Poor Mama. Ever since last Christmas, when she'd met Dave, she'd been giving Nikki subtle and not-so-subtle hints. Mama liked him. His people hadn't come *apo tin patrida*—from your country—

meaning Greece, but he would fit right into the family. With Nikki's sister Iris dead, Nikki was Mama's only hope she would ever attend a child's wedding. Iris had never given her parents that pleasure, had been rebellious from the first, had conceived Lara out of wedlock two years before she'd become sick with the fatal leukemia. Nikki felt bad for her mother but wished that for right now Mama would stop pushing her. She was about to put the letter back into its envelope when she noticed that the paragraph about the wedding dress had been bracketed with green ballpoint.

Lara! Nikki felt as though she were being bombarded. She shut the light and staggered into her bedroom. Two A.M. She set the alarm for five, lay down and was asleep in minutes.

# 12

The parking lot looked the same as it had yesterday, except that the Mercedes was gone now and so were the cops and crowds of people. At 0730 hours on another frigid morning, the sun was playing hide-and-seek behind the clouds again. Nikki walked from the unused office building to the gate closing off the walkway planking, hands in the pockets of her jacket, not knowing what had brought her here. She felt a deep uneasiness, as though she were missing something important.

After fifteen minutes she still had no clue. Why had Zaporelli ended up here? It was an ideal spot to dump a body, deserted for the most part. Had the killer known the place or driven around looking for this kind of location? If he'd known where he was headed, that hinted at premeditation. Otherwise, it might have been a crime of impulse, an argument gone out of control, an unplanned act of violence, the killer driving around afterward, looking for a place to leave the corpse.

She tried reconstructing the crime from the killer's point of view, pacing from one end of the cyclone fence to the other. She patched together the pieces she had and filled in the blanks with educated guesses. It had been seven o'clock or thereabouts on a Tuesday evening. They'd been parked on the side of a quiet street. The perp had shot Zaporelli. No one had heard the shot—if the windows were closed, the sound wouldn't have carried. Then Zaporelli was shoved over to the passenger seat while his murderer drove around and found this place. A second shot, and then the killer had gone home, or somewhere.

She came to a halt. How had the killer left the scene? Walked? Was it a local person, someone who lived in one of the houses nearby? Was she wasting her time with Zaporelli's wife, mistress, those he'd been close to—should she be rereading the reports on neighborhood people, looking for a clue she'd missed?

She left the parking lot and started walking away from the water toward Gerritsen Avenue, where she'd parked the Camaro. If the killer *hadn't* been local, he'd have had to figure out how to get out of this lonely corner of Brooklyn. Not many cabs cruised this area, but she could check them. If he'd hailed a cab, there'd be a record. The driver might remember him, come up with a description. She'd have someone call the regular cab companies and check the gypsies, or unlicensed cabs.

What if the killer had had his own car? He could have driven away. That would mean he'd come here in *his* car, not Zaporelli's. Or he'd met Zaporelli in Brooklyn, waited for him somewhere. She didn't like the feel of the two-car theory. It was clumsy and didn't have the simplicity of real life.

But that left her with the same question. If there had been one car, how had the killer left the scene?

She got into the Camaro, forgetting in her concentration how low to the ground it was. She felt jolted as she hit the seat, as though she'd sat on the floor suddenly. Someday, because she'd been taken in by the low-slung, glamorous look of the Camaro, she'd be an orthopedic patient. Over the four years she'd owned the car she'd probably thrown every bone of her six-foot frame out of whack crawling in and out of it.

She pulled out onto Gerritsen, stopped for a light. On the corner was a bus stop. Public transportation—why hadn't she thought of it? The perp could have made the hit, walked six blocks, then taken the Gerritsen bus away from the scene.

She would question the drivers on the route. You never knew when you'd get lucky.

# 13

Nikki and Stavich watched Dr. Lonny Chi, Assistant Medical Examiner for the city of New York, extract a bullet from what had been Dean Zaporelli's groin with a pair of long-handled forceps. Autopsies weren't easy for Nikki, even after five of them. It wasn't as though she attended two or three a week. The 168th precinct was fairly tame, unlike East New York or Bedford-Stuyvesant. She had her worst moments when the horizontal cut was made across the skull and the pathologist snapped open the brain cavity. The problem was not the way it looked but the popping sound. It vibrated through every part of her.

Stavich, experienced as he was, had had his difficult moments this morning. She'd caught him swallowing hard as Chi crunched his way through the corpse's breastbone, using a pair of cutters. Stavich had seemed to develop a sudden curiosity about the time and had looked down at his watch in spite of the wall clock directly in his line of vision.

Chi clicked off the overhead mike now. "This slug's in better shape than the one from his head," he remarked. He dropped the slug into a plastic bag. "But the first one is the one that did it, took him right out."

"Head on?" Nikki asked.

"As far as I can see."

Chi handed the bag to Nikki. The bullet's metal jacket gleamed through the plastic.

Stavich said, "An automatic—I told ya the .38 wasn't the gun."

The metal meant the bullet had most likely come from an automatic. The glove-compartment gun had been a revolver, a .38. "If the perp didn't use that .38," Nikki said, "why was it in the car?"

"Who knows?" A fresh cigarette lay behind Stavich's ear, gleaming white under the fluorescent.

Chi switched on the mike again and described the groin wound and the bullet. He finished cutting, weighing, measuring the rest of the body and handed the bagged samples to Nikki and Stavich to be labeled.

The head wound had been delivered, Chi had told them, from within two feet. There had been the grayish stippling of powder burns around the entry, visible once the blood was cleared.

Her close-range theory was correct; the killer might be someone Zaporelli knew well. She remembered two reports she'd read this morning—the first was the BCI check on Karen Royce. Karen had never served any jail time, had no sheet. The second was a rundown of Karen's whereabouts on Tuesday evening. She'd been out of her apartment at the time of the murder. In a follow-up check, detectives would question the doorman of her building, the garage attendant. Nikki remembered how shaken Karen had been the morning after the murder and made a mental note to question her again.

Chi's glasses started slipping down his nose. He moved them up with a rubber-gloved finger and delivered his windup speech to the microphone. He had "examined this body, opened and examined the above-noted cavities and organs as recorded, and in my opinion the cause of death was a bullet wound in the region of the skull—"

The .38 Colt troubled Nikki. Why had it been in the car? An unnecessary item, like a fifth leg on a dog. She said to Stavich as they waited for the elevator, "There were no bullets for that

.38. Not in Zaporelli's apartment, nowhere in his office. Unless he hid them somewhere real good. Our guys turned everything upside down."

"Didya ever think the bullets're in someone?" Stavich said. "Maybe a floater shows up in the river next week and he's got .38 slugs in him and they match."

"I don't think so. If Zaporelli killed someone with the gun, why leave it around in plain sight?"

The elevator came. They squeezed in among a crowd of white-coated personnel. The smell of disinfectant was sickeningly strong.

Nikki was only marginally aware of the smell. Her brain was busy with the autopsy findings. The killer had used an automatic—there must have been spent shell casings after the gun had been fired. But none had been found. The perp had stopped to pick up the casings after the hit.

Number one, the killer knew enough about guns to look for the casings. Number two, he had the presence of mind to remember to collect them. Neat and organized. But cool, too. Almost like a professional, but not quite. No barrage of bullets to whack the victim with a massive blast of firepower. No "disappearance" of the body into newly laid concrete.

But the killer was someone who'd had experience. Someone who'd probably killed before.

She took a cab to Zaporelli's building. Stavich had gone back to SoHo on Glenn Taylor's trail, hoping Glenn would lead him to Matt. Thirty-six hours had passed since Matt had last been seen. Nikki felt uneasy when she thought about him, edgier with each passing minute.

In the marble lobby the harried young man with the corrugated forehead glared at her from behind the desk. His gold epaulets reflected the red of his uniform, looking like anemic worms someone had dumped on his shoulder. "I thought the police were finished," he said.

"There's been a murder. Or haven't you heard?"

His mouth screwed into a tight twist. "You wish to see Mrs. Zaporelli?"

"No." She fished in her purse for a copy of the DD5 she'd brought from the station and found the name of Zaporelli's neighbor. "Dr. Carpenter."

"Sixteen J."

He lifted his hand in an arc above the desk bell, ready to summon a red-jacket for Nikki's trip through the lobby, but she said, "Thanks, I can find it myself," and walked through the Arabian Nights decor to the elevator.

She scanned the DD5 report as the car rose. Dr. Carpenter, Zaporelli's neighbor, had said during the canvass interview that on the day of the murder she'd overheard a fight next door.

The elevator doors slid open. In the mirrored entry foyer, the boy who reminded her of her father still sat on the rocks, staring across the water. Her father had been young when he'd left Greece, only fifteen. He and his brothers had been fishermen there, but her father was the only one who'd gone back to fishing in the new country.

She turned her back on the Zaporellis' door and pressed the bell opposite. She would see Donna and Elaine later, but first she wanted to hear their neighbor's story.

A tall, spare woman in her eighties answered. She wore a cashmere sweater frayed at the collar, a tweed skirt. Her hair, a white, wispy taffy-pull, was caught loosely at the back of her head. She glanced at Nikki's ID. "Come in," she said, holding the door wide.

The rooms were identical to Zaporelli's in reverse position, like the opposite wings of a butterfly, but much less luxuriously furnished. Nikki noticed the shabbiness right away, the struggle to maintain appearances. The fringe on the entry carpet had torn and been sewn amateurishly. The porcelain umbrella stand showed cracks where it had been mended.

Dr. Carpenter led Nikki into a living room that needed paint. She sat on a sofa and gestured toward a chair.

Nikki said, "You told the police you overheard a fight on Tuesday."

"That's right."

"At about what time?"

She squinted, the folds of her skin gathering then relaxing in a network of wrinkles. "About five."

"What kind of fight? People yelling—or using their fists?"

"Both. I was right here reading and I heard a commotion. He—Mr. Zaporelli—was blasting away at the top of his lungs. I couldn't hear the other man clearly. There was scuffling—I felt bad afterward that I didn't call the police. I heard someone land against the wall, as though he'd been thrown. Then a woman screamed—I think it was Mrs. Zaporelli—'You bastard! Look what you did!' There had been a lot of noise generally Tuesday afternoon—Mr. and Mrs. Zaporelli had had a shouting match earlier."

The phone rang. Dr. Carpenter excused herself and went to the foyer to answer it. She came back a moment later. "It's for you," she said to Nikki.

It was Dave. "Can I see you? I'm downstairs in the lobby."

Her stomach tensed, lost its grounding. "I was going to see Mrs. Zaporelli after this."

"It won't take long."

"Be down in a little while."

She hung up. What was important enough to make him seek her out in the middle of her workday? He'd never done that before. Now she was sorry she'd agreed to meet him, afraid that what he might say would further disrupt her.

"Dr. Carpenter," she said, forcing herself back to the case, "you were saying the Zaporellis had had a fight earlier on Tuesday afternoon. What was that about?"

"She said she was fed up, that something or other was the

final straw. She must have threatened him in some way, because he said, 'Just you go ahead and try it.'"

"You recognized their voices?"

"I know their voices. We've spoken in the lobby and elevator. And of course I heard him a lot on television."

"You were never really friendly."

Dr. Carpenter ran a strong, square finger along the couch arm. Her hands were well developed. Nikki wondered if she'd been a surgeon, if that was why she was called *doctor*. "I knew their maids better. I do my own wash—I'm one of the few tenants who does. So I've met their maids in the laundry room. The last one was a talker."

"She talked about the family?"

Dr. Carpenter glanced at a tug steaming by on the East River. "I hate gossip."

Nikki murmured, "This is a murder. If you know anything that might help us—"

"Well—it seems he liked the ladies. Couldn't keep his hands off them—some men can't, you know. Before he got what's-her-name—that woman who takes care of Mrs. Zaporelli now—"

"Miss Lessing?"

"Yes, before he got her he had this knockout nurse, and she spent most of her time trying to stay in her uniform. So finally Mrs. Zaporelli fired the girl and hired this cold fish they have now."

"You don't particularly like Miss Lessing."

"I don't have much to do with her." Her eyes flashed angrily.

"Did something happen?"

"It was only a small—I have this tendon in my arm that bothers me—sometimes without warning. If I carry anything I'm in agony. I was walking up Third Avenue with a bag of groceries and it suddenly went out. I put the bag on the sidewalk and this Lessing person came by wheeling a wire cart. I said hello and explained about my arm. I asked her would she mind if I put my bag in. She said no, she couldn't stop. Just shook her head and walked past. Didn't even say she was sorry. I haven't said a word to her since." She rubbed her arm, as though the memory had activated the pain again, then shrugged. "It's not very charitable of me to hold the grudge— maybe she was just preoccupied."

"You said you recognized Mr. Zaporelli's voice yesterday. What did he say?"

The wrinkles on her forehead deepened. "He said, 'I never heard of the Land of Light.'" She laughed. "Weird, isn't it? He also said, 'There is no Tony Zim. Forget Tony Zim.' Make any sense to you?"

"Not yet." As Nikki scribbled the sentences into her notebook she remembered a name she'd seen yesterday in the article in Glenn Taylor's loft. "Could he have said, 'Lantern Light'? 'I never heard of the Lantern Light'?"

"That's it. Exactly."

Nikki rose. "Thanks very much." As they walked to the door she noticed Dr. Carpenter was almost her height. She might have been even taller before she'd aged. Nikki liked to measure herself against other tall women.

Dr. Carpenter looked troubled as they said good bye. "Not my habit to repeat what people say," she pointed out.

"These are special circumstances."

"I hope it helps."

Dave was in the lobby on a couch near one of the balloon lamps. He rose as she approached, and they stood together awkwardly. She waited for him to ask her to sit or come out to lunch with him, but he did neither. The young red-jacket with the ridged forehead glanced their way uneasily as though he too was uncomfortable about their meeting.

"I wanted to tell you," Dave said, "I won't be able to see you. I didn't want to just disappear."

"What does that mean? You're going to avoid me? What if the case—"

"It has nothing to do with the job. I mean one-on-one situations. What happened last night was no good for me." The kiss—he meant their kiss though he wasn't saying it, the fact that she'd stopped him, had held him off. "I can't handle it right now."

"I thought you weren't going to pressure me," she said.

"It's not pressure—"

"You're saying you won't see me until I—"

"I'm saying I can't." He took a step away from her, looked back. "Okay?"

"Do I have a choice?"

He didn't answer.

She stared at his retreating back. She should feel grateful. After all, this was what she'd asked for—space and time to think. Yet she felt as though he'd abandoned her; it couldn't have come at a worse time.

# 14

Donna herself opened the door of 16K. Nikki was relieved. She'd expected Elaine Lessing to be guarding the place like Cerberus, the watchdog at the gates of hell in the Greek myths she read to Lara.

Donna glanced behind Nikki, as though looking for someone else. "You find my son?"

"Not yet. We have a bulletin out."

Her lips flattened into a straight line. "A bulletin!" she sneered. She gripped the knob tightly and held the door half-shut. She looked younger out of bed, attractive in designer jeans and a pale silk blouse that emphasized her sultry skin. Her figure showed well, full breasts and rounded hips, cinched-in waist. "Why didn't they announce you, anyhow? What kind of security is it if—"

"I came into the building earlier, to see one of your neighbors."

"Oh God—talk about washing your dirty linen in public! When is this gonna end? How do I get rid of you?"

"You could try telling the truth, for starters."

"What?" She glared at Nikki. "Listen, Miss—I want your name and badge number—"

"Mrs. Zaporelli, if we pussyfoot around, it's going to take forever. You lied to us yesterday. I have a pretty good idea why."

Donna loosened her grip on the knob.

"Matt was here the day his father died, wasn't he?"

The fight went out of her face, taking some of the color with it.

Nikki said, "You going to ask me in, or you want to do this in the hall?"

She let Nikki into the apartment. Her eyes had a haunted look, as though she hadn't slept in days. "I don't want Matty mixed up in this."

"He is already."

"What d'you mean?"

"He had a fight with your husband the day of the murder. People overheard him."

"So?"

"He went down afterward and said he was going to kill him."

Donna stepped backward. Nikki thought she would lose her footing and tumble down the steps into the living room, but she reeled against the wall instead, holding on to the cherry-wood desk. "You don't know what you're talking about! Matty didn't kill Dean. He didn't kill anyone. He couldn't!"

"How come you're so sure? You know who did?"

Her eyes narrowed. "It's just— It's not in his nature. If you knew him, you'd see."

The phone rang. Donna moved toward it awkwardly, snatching it up. "Yes?" Her eyes were bright with worry. An instant later her features settled into the familiar lines of disappointment as she recognized the caller. "I'll get back to you," she said in a flat tone. She hung up and said sadly to Nikki, "I keep thinking Matty'll call."

"Tell me about the fight he had with your husband yesterday. Where was it—upstairs?"

"No. They were right here."

"You were here too?"

Her glance shifted off Nikki's, then back again, as though

she were deciding what to say. "I was in bed. I heard Dean let him in."

"About what time?"

"Somewhere around four thirty. Elaine had gone out just before. I remember thinking Dean had asked for the car at five thirty, and when I heard them start in on each other I looked at the clock and wondered whether Dean was gonna be late."

"What were they fighting about?"

"The usual. Matty wanted the money his grandfather left him and his father said no way, not till you get a job."

"How much money are we talking about?"

"I'm not even sure—close to a million, I think. Matty was supposed to get it when he turned eighteen last August. But Dean screwed around with the estate so it ended up *he* controlled it. And he wouldn't give him a nickel. Dean didn't want him to be a singer—he said the kid was an embarrassment to him. Singing is all Matty cares about. I used to tell Dean, history repeats itself. Dean was gonna be an actor when he was young—and *his* father was against it. But he didn't want to know any of that."

"Your husband was in the theater?"

"I'm not sure—he coulda been." Some dark, private thought made her flush. She let go of the desk and slumped into a chair in front of it. "He led his own life." She studied the arm of the chair as though it held a clue to the puzzle of her life. "I didn't know him long when we married. Let me tell you, he was *gorgeous*. Not handsome—*gorgeous*. And smart, just out of college. His father owned a construction company, so he had the dough to wine and dine me. I was seventeen—what'd I know? My mother saw what he was, all for himself. That's not the kind'll make you happy, Donna, she said. Did I listen?" Her glance turned inward, connected with the waste of years, the disillusion. "From day one he had other women. When I asked him he laughed, or he'd yell at me to stay outta his life. Some nights he didn't even come home. Some marriage!" She rubbed her knee

with a fingertip. The nail had been filed to fashionable blunt-
ness, polished to a rosy glow. "I was gonna leave him. But when
Matty came, I wanted a regular life for him, a family. Not that
Dean was around much. But I thought, I love the baby enough
for both of us—he'll be okay." Sadness weighed down her features, deepening the lines from nose to mouth, the creases at
the corners of her eyes. "The kid had trouble from the word go."

"What kind of trouble?"

"He was miserable. He didn't want to go to school, he was
scared to leave the house. He was so bad it even seemed to get
through to his father. When Matty was five Dean like, changed.
Started staying home nights, shaved off his mustache, settled
down. He went to law school like his father always wanted. I
thought, great, he's growing up." She swallowed. "It didn't last.
A kid needs parents who respect each other. Dean treated me
like shit. The day he died he took a call right in my bedroom,
not two feet away from me—I could tell it was that bimbo he
keeps, the Royce slut. He was talking to her like she mattered,
like she wasn't just a high-class whore."

"According to her, she loved him," Nikki said.

"*Love*! She wouldn't know the meaning of the word. She
*screwed* Dean—and I don't mean in bed. Told tales outta
school, spied on him. A nasty piece of work, always looking
out for her own good." She pointed a finger at Nikki. "And she
better not hold a grudge against you. She waits for her chance
and then sticks it to you, gets even." She stopped, seeming suddenly aware that she'd said more than she wanted to. "Anyhow, that's who he was talking to."

"What was he saying?"

She hesitated. "Who listened? I just heard the sound of his
voice."

And yet Dr. Carpenter had said Donna had threatened Zaporelli, had called something "the final straw." She decided to
send up a trial balloon. "He was planning to marry her, you
know."

Donna looked at her in surprise, then threw her head back and laughed. "Is that what he told her? Poor little Goldilocks! Serves her right if she believed him. You tell her if she wants the list of all the girls he promised to marry, I'll be glad to help her out. Nineteen years of his shenanigans!" A fire blazed in her eyes. "I told him, 'The least you can do is take your private calls elsewhere. I don't have to hear them.' He looked at me like what're you gonna do about it? And then he had this huge fight with Matty—World War Three. It was too much. I thought—" She swallowed hard. "God forgive me, when I saw him down at the Medical Examiner's yesterday, only part of me was sorry."

"Did Matt ask him about a theater called the Lantern Light?"

"Yeah—what was all that? Dean said he never heard of it. He blew up and gave it to Matty both barrels. I got outta bed then. I figured let me come down before they kill each other. It took me a while—I was moving slow that day."

"Was Tony Zim mentioned?"

She nodded. "Dean didn't know him either. Then Matty said something I couldn't hear. I was back by the stairs. Next thing I know, there's wrestling—furniture's sliding around, stuff's falling. I run in here and Dean's got the kid by the throat—he's slapping him around." Her hand cut the air. "I was ready to go back up for my cane—I could of killed the bastard—" She stopped suddenly, realizing what she'd said. She added in a quieter tone, "But Matty pulled away and ran out before I could do anything."

A key turned in the lock. Elaine Lessing opened the door. She wore a white-and-black tweed coat that seemed to continue the pepper and salt of her hair. Her large, old-fashioned collar was buttoned as though she'd been cold. She pulled her keys from the lock and held them uncertainly, looking at Nikki, her forehead creasing. "I didn't know you'd be back."

"I told you I might."

Donna cut in. "What took you so long?"

"They didn't have the black ones," Elaine said. "They had every color but that."

"What'd you buy?"

"Nothing. I wasn't sure—"

"*Nothing*? Shit! What'm I supposed to wear?"

"I'll go out again, Donna. It's only—"

"Forget it!" She pulled herself out of the chair and sailed toward the staircase, dark hair billowing behind her like a storm cloud. Nikki, remembering how stiffly she'd moved yesterday, was surprised by her agility. She wondered if Donna's doctor had called in. He'd gone to Cancun on vacation three days ago, had been expected to pick up messages this morning and get in touch with the precinct.

Elaine ran after Donna as far as the staircase. "I'll go out again, Donna. I don't mind."

"*Forget* it. Leave me alone now." Her footsteps sounded on the staircase. A minute later a door slammed somewhere on the floor above.

Elaine came back, pale cheeks tinged with color, and unbuttoned her coat. "She isn't always like this. It's her son. She's worried—" She let the sentence hang unfinished. She took off her coat, opened a nearby closet, pulled out a hanger.

Nikki said, "I spoke to his roommate, Glenn. He told me how they met."

She looked at Nikki quickly and said in a thick whisper, "Then you know about—that he tried to do away with himself." She had a slow, fussy way of speaking, not the rapid-fire rhythm of a New Yorker.

"Miss Lessing, why did he try to commit suicide?"

"It was a week before his birthday, last summer. He was looking forward to getting out of the house. He wanted so much to be independent. When he found out his father wasn't planning to give him an inheritance that was coming to him, he took every pill in the house, and then some." She glanced upward, in the direction of Donna's bedroom. "She's afraid this whole thing'll set him off again, that he won't be able to handle it. She's been out of her mind since he disappeared."

"*I* may have upset her today," Nikki said. "I asked about Karen Royce."

At the mention of Karen's name Elaine straightened up and concentrated on the coat again. She put it on the hanger, closed the top button.

"Miss Royce called here on Tuesday, didn't she?"

"Yes. I put the call through to Mr. Zaporelli."

"I understand there was quite a blowup."

Elaine didn't answer, suddenly having difficulty fitting the hanger over the clothes rod. Nikki said, "Mrs. Zaporelli told me she felt Mr. Zaporelli had gone too far this time. That it was the final straw."

She turned full face toward Nikki. "Donna's a sainted angel! She's shared her husband with that woman for years! Back home they'd call her—they'd have a name for a woman like her."

"Where's home?"

"Cincinnati." She blinked. "Not bad enough he spends— spent—days and nights with her—he supported her, too. Three thousand dollars a month. In cash, you understand, so nothing would show. That was to make sure she didn't have to pay taxes on it. He covered her rent, her clothes, whatever." She lowered her voice. "She always *was* a gold digger—I watched her when we worked together. She sucked him dry— whatever she could get. Plus she drew a neat salary as his campaign manager. Believe me, she didn't have money worries." She swung the closet door shut. "I ought to know—I used to call the bank the fourth Tuesday of every month to tell them to have her money ready. She would pick it up herself."

"You called this past Tuesday?"

"That's right." She smirked. "He once told me the money was for relatives, but I wasn't fooled. Who else would he have given it to?"

"His mother, maybe—didn't he go there regularly?"

She shook her head. "His mother had more than he did. She didn't need it."

"What bank was it?"

"Federated National, the branch at Broadway and Thirty-ninth. In the same building where the Metropolitan Opera used to be."

Nikki noted the information in her book. She would call the precinct and have someone get a subpoena from the DA's office for a printout of Zaporelli's bank records. And it wouldn't hurt to question Karen Royce about the three thousand dollars Zaporelli withdrew from his account every month.

A door opened above and Donna called, "Elaine!"

Elaine said, "I'd better go," and ushered Nikki out.

She waited for the elevator. The boy in the mirror hadn't moved from his perch on the rocks, but her mind was taken up with other things.

Karen Royce had picked up three thousand dollars on Tuesday. If she'd handed the money to Zaporelli and he'd had it in his possession at the time of the murder, it could have been a motive. That had been Stavich's theory from the start— a straight-up robbery. But if it had been that, why shoot the man between the legs after he was dead? Why leave a two-thousand-dollar watch on his wrist?

In the elevator she made a mistake, pressing the button marked G, thinking it was Ground. It turned out to be Garage. Too late, she noticed the L for Lobby just above it.

She stepped into the whitewashed garage and waved to the manager, holding up her badge to remind him of who she was. Now that she was here, she might as well follow the route Zaporelli's car would have taken as it left the building.

She took a walkway up the ramp that led to the street and peered out into a light drizzle. A stoplight faced the exit. A car pulled up, a long, sleek Corvette, even lower to the ground than her Camaro. A beauty—what was it in her that was drawn to ground-hugging cars? A secret yearning to be short? Not to have been the tallest in every class at school, even counting the boys?

The Corvette stopped at the light, waiting till it turned green. Nikki timed the light—forty seconds.

She watched the Corvette pull away. Both the garage manager and his assistant had said Zaporelli was alone when he'd driven out on Tuesday. But anyone could have waited for him at the garage exit. In forty seconds anyone could have entered the car.

# 15

Chief Dritzer perched on the edge of Eagle-Eye's desk, fluorescent light bouncing off his polished scalp. "Where the hell's the son?"

He looked at Eagle-Eye, and Eagle-Eye looked at Nikki. "Stavich had a lead to him," she said, "but it fizzled."

Stavich took a deep breath. He'd aged visibly in the past twenty-four hours, the flesh beneath his eyes sagging. "I been running my ass off. This Taylor guy—the roommate? He don't sleep—all he does is run around looking for the kid."

Dritzer stood, a muscle working in the side of his jaw. "Thirty-six hours since Zaporelli got hit. What're we *doing* here? I mean, what the hell are we doing?" He turned to Eagle-Eye.

Matt's picture had been distributed widely, shown on TV. The homeless shelters had been checked; cops on the beat had shaken men sleeping on the street, shone lights into their faces. A sudden thought disturbed Nikki—was Matt okay? Was he just hiding because he was frightened or had something happened to him so that he wasn't able to come forward?

Dritzer leaned toward Eagle-Eye. "You want more cops? The whole goddamn department's not enough?"

Eagle-Eye squinted up from behind his desk. He looked like someone had done a bad assembly job on his face, putting his eyes in the wrong place, too close to his nose.

Dritzer said, "I have a three o'clock appointment to see the Commissioner, tell him everything's running smooth. *You* go lie to him!" He paced to the window. "You got an unstable kid. A kid with a motive. He *ran away*, for God's sake. What more do you need?"

He marched to the door and put chunky fingers on the knob. Nikki felt a surge of relief at the thought that he might finally go. He was the last of the brass to leave today's conference—the Chief of Detectives had put in a token appearance; the District Duty Captain had spent a half hour estimating the size of her bra, checking the fit of her panty hose.

Dritzer glared at Eagle-Eye. "If nothing moves by tomorrow, we'll make some changes around here."

"I understand," Eagle-Eye said.

"I thought you would." The door shut behind Dritzer with a dull thunk.

Eagle-Eye massaged the bridge of his nose with his thumb and forefinger. "Well, boys and girls, any questions?"

Stavich pulled out a Camel, caught Eagle-Eye's glance and tucked it behind his ear.

"What're we supposed to do," Nikki said, "produce the Zaporelli kid out of thin air? We put out a bulletin, set up a hot line—these things take time."

"You had a whole day." Eagle-Eye pointed a pencil at her. "Go back to where the kid lives. Climb up this Taylor creep's ass. Don't let him outta sight."

"There's another possibility," Nikki said. "When we were at the kid's place there was a magazine article on a theater, the Lantern Light. Taylor saw me reading it and grabbed it away like it was a million bucks he'd lost somewhere."

"So? There you go, off on some wild-goose chase."

"Zaporelli's neighbor, the one who heard the fight, told me the kid said something about the Lantern Light to his father. The wife corrobs that."

"Why the hell didn't you say so?"

I just did, Nikki felt like answering.

Stavich sat up straighter. "The Lantern Light. That's where

the Chase guy worked—the Nose-Job case." His eyes slitted. "Here's a guy who's dead already and the perp gives him a fin- ish-off, right in the nose."

Nikki felt her adrenalin flow. For an instant she couldn't speak. "Like Zaporelli," she pointed out.

Eagle-Eye dropped the pencil onto his desk. "Listen, Trakos, the Nose-Job case was six years ago. Don't get your ass in an uproar. You want to go down to this Lantern place, okay. But don't waste time digging up this other shit. It's too old. Bring me the Zaporelli kid. Yesterday, if not sooner."

As soon as Eagle-Eye's door had shut Nikki asked Stavich, "What do you remember about Chase?"

"The Nose Job? Not a hell of a lot. Lawton caught it."

Somehow she'd known it would come to this—that she'd be forced to call Dave if she wanted to get on with the case. Would he help her with this one? Of course he would. He was too good a cop to let personal matters interfere with the job. So why did she feel uncomfortable asking for his help?

She moved toward her phone but Stavich asked, "Can I make a call? I gotta let the wife know I'm not comin' home again tonight."

She went through the papers on her desk while he dialed. "Hello, honey? I'm staying here again." Pause. "I *know* it's two nights in a row. Whaddaya want *me* to do? A guy got killed."

Police marriages were battlegrounds. Didn't Dave know that? The divorce rate was incredibly high. Long hours on the job, emotional exhaustion from the nature of the work, partic- ularly homicide—nothing was left when there *was* time. Why did Dave want to take a relationship that was fun and exciting and turn it into a dull round of commitment and obligation?

Donna Zaporelli's doctor, Leon Fishberg, had called in. Donna had a form of rheumatoid arthritis. On some days her abilities were almost normal; in fact the doctor *would* call them normal. She could do tasks that required finger dexterity—

cooking, for instance. How about tasks that required strength, like pulling a trigger? Nikki was sorry the cop who'd spoken to him hadn't asked him that. She made a note to call Fishberg again.

Jameson, at the next desk, had been calling cab companies to find out if any of their cars had picked up a passenger two nights ago at the crime scene. She heard him say, "Thank you very much. Take my number, just in case."

He hung up and said to Nikki in his sweet West Indian lilt, "Mon, do you know how many cab companies there are in Brooklyn?" A tray of deviled egg halves with strange salmon-colored filling lay on his desk. He popped one into his mouth, offered Nikki another. She shook her head. "And that is not counting gypsies, either."

She'd have someone check the gypsy cabs. What made her feel she was wasting time, that the killer wouldn't have left the scene in a taxi? "Any luck with the regular companies?" she asked.

"Not so far. Many of them do not go into that area to look for a fare after dark. Too lonely."

"It could have been a cab that had dropped someone off and was headed home."

"I will keep calling."

A report on her desk showed that Karen Royce, Zaporelli's girlfriend, had lied when she'd told Nikki she'd gone home at about three thirty or four and stayed there. The report covered an interview with Karen's doorman and some of the building personnel. Karen had come in at two. The doorman had buzzed her at four fifteen when a package came for her, but no one had answered. She'd picked up her car at three thirty and had come back into the building at half-past nine, carrying two bottles of Scotch. When she'd signed for her package, the doorman noted, her hand shook so badly it had been hard to recognize her writing.

Stavich said into the phone, "I'm sorry. I forgot it was his birthday. No, go ahead without me. I'll call and talk to him later. Okay, honey. Me too." He hung up. "Pain in the ass," he muttered as he shuffled out the door. "I'm goin' back to SoHo."

Dave was out, she discovered when she called his office, but he'd left a number where he could be reached. When he answered she heard a rumble in the background. "Where are you?"

"In the subway. Someone left a stiff down here, on a bench in the Hoyt Street station. What's up?"

"Stavich told me you worked on the Nose-Job case—"

"Chase. Yeah, a long time ago." Even with the noise of an approaching train she could hear the disappointment in his voice. He'd been hoping she'd come to a decision about the two of them. "What about it?"

She waited till the train had passed. "There might be a connection to Zaporelli. Can you meet me?"

A station loudspeaker boomed, drowned his answer. "What'd you say?"

"I said okay." He didn't sound enthusiastic. Or was it the background noise that made his voice so flat? "How about the Yemeni?" he said.

The place was rich with memory—did he realize that? They'd eaten there the first night they'd made love, enjoyed a leisurely meal of Middle-Eastern specialties, gotten high on white zinfandel, absorbed the sensual decor for hours before they finally made their way to his apartment. She hesitated, but for some reason didn't say no, didn't suggest another place. "Five thirty," she said.

# 16

A rehearsal was underway when she arrived at the Lantern Light. A bear of a man, tall and broad with thick, unruly hair, directed a woman in a scene on the lighted stage. "I'm not at all sure California's the answer," the actress said.

"You've almost got it, darling," the big man said. "Try it again." His voice was surprisingly gentle for his size.

Nikki stood inside the curtain that screened the dark theater from the lobby. The street door had been open, though this wasn't the safest part of the city, on the edge of Chelsea, in the shadow of an unused railroad overpass. It was an area that housed auto-repair companies, collision shops, and parking garages, though a few off-off Broadway companies had taken over some of the empty buildings. No one had stopped Nikki as she'd walked through the lobby with its threadbare carpet, homemade ticket boxes, and old production photos and into the theater itself.

She cleared her throat and the big man whirled and peered into the shadows. "May I help you?"

She walked forward. He was imposing up close, taller than her six feet by four or five inches. His white shirt had pulled loose from his jeans as though there wasn't enough cloth to contain him. His beard was thick and full, gray here and there though he couldn't have been more than forty.

Nikki showed her badge. He didn't change expression. "I'm

Peter Maynard, director and manager of this establishment."
He said to the actress, "Take a break, darling." His voice was
rich and full, trained.

"This way," he said. "I think we'll be more comfortable."
He led her to a tiny office beyond the lobby, with barely
enough room for two chairs and a high, old-fashioned desk.
Papers, scripts, and pictures lay stacked on the back shelf.

A framed photograph of a man dominated the room.
*Bernard Seymour Chase*, the legend read. Round-faced and
soft-featured, he smiled beneath a flop of fair hair. She remembered his face from the article she'd seen in Glenn Taylor's loft. Oddly, she felt as though she'd seen him someplace
else but couldn't recall where. She gestured toward the photo,
said, "He was murdered, wasn't he?"

"Yes." Sorrow pulled down his mouth and made his face
seem longer. "He founded the Lantern years ago, gave me my
first job."

Nikki let the moment go by. "I'm here about Dean Zaporelli's murder, Mr. Maynard."

"Ah." His hair made him look like a teddy bear, but his eyes
were sharp, even cunning. "What makes you think *I* can help
you?"

"Did you know Zaporelli?"

"No." The slightest hesitation. Then, "His son was here
about a week ago. I came in at ten one morning and he was
outside. He's a funny kid."

"What do you mean?"

"Kind of pathetic. He looked so grubby I thought he was
homeless. Then he opened his mouth and told me who he was.
He was in a state—I had the feeling he'd been sitting out there
for hours."

Again Nikki felt worried for Matt. He was the kind of kid
who didn't cope well with the "real" world. "What did he
want?" she asked.

"He wasn't sure. Someone had sent him a note telling him

to come here. He showed it to me—something like, 'Go down to the Lantern Light, learn about Tony Zim.'"

"Tony Zim?"

"Zim was co-founder of the place, Bernie Chase's partner. He was involved at the very beginning, but he dropped out when all the trouble started."

"I saw a magazine article—"

"My friend wrote that piece—he's a publicist. He said people would be curious, would come to see where it all happened." He laughed. "I have to admit it's worked. We don't have standing room, but business is better."

"When did the article come out?"

"Two, three weeks ago. Want a copy?"

"Please."

He stood and leaned over the desk, rummaging through a stack on the shelf. "I have a bunch here somewhere—" His shirt pulled free of his jeans, revealing a band of tan and some inches of the line between his buttocks. Nikki cast around for a safe place to look. On the opposite wall hung a collection of framed awards and certificates made out in the name of Bernard Seymour Chase. She was about to look back when she saw a familiar document—a diploma from Brown University, a twin of the one she'd seen in Zaporelli's apartment.

"Here it is," Maynard said, handing her the reprint. He hitched up his pants and sat down.

She skimmed the article and read again about the girl whose body had been found "among the trash bags on Little West Twelfth Street. Lisa Hirsch had turned sixteen the week before."

Nikki said, "She was just a teenager, this Hirsch girl."

"Yes, a tragedy. People remembered—they called and wrote. It seems the girl's mother refused to believe it when the police called it accidental death—she picketed the mayor's office, got written up in the papers." His lips flattened into a straight line. "I know how she felt. When Bernie was killed, I was furious with the police—they weren't looking hard enough; they'd shoved the case into a corner and were letting it rot. When the article came out, some new leads surfaced. Last week I got a card from a private detective in Brooklyn who said he had some information." He fished in a drawer, handed her a business card.

*Reuben Bienstock*, Nikki read. *Criminal, Industrial, Matrimonial. Confidential. Free Consultation.*

"Did you tell the police about this?" she asked.

There was a flutter of calculation behind his eyes. "Yes, of course. I spoke to the detective in charge of the case—a man named Lawton. Nice enough man, but I doubt much will happen."

Nikki copied Bienstock's address into her book and glanced up to find Maynard looking at her oddly. He said, "I suppose when I saw your badge I was hoping you'd come about Bernie."

"You were close?"

"He was my mentor, my brother, my father. I didn't have a place to stay and my wife was pregnant at the time. He let us use some rooms at the theater till we got settled. He had his own problems, but he liked me—and we both loved the theater—that was his life." The tips of his nostrils were pale and tight. "I hate to think the son of a bitch who killed him is walking around free, enjoying life."

She hadn't been aware of the rage under his gentleness, guessed it had been feeding on itself since the death of his friend. "I'm sorry, Mr. Maynard," she said.

She slid her notebook into her purse. "What exactly is your job here?" she asked.

It took a moment for him to focus on what she'd said, as though he'd traveled to some distant place inside himself. She had the feeling he would rather have gone on about Chase. "My job?" He laughed. "Let me try to describe it. I baby-sit the actors, plunge the toilets when they get stuck—"

"You're here every night?"

"Whenever there's a show." He hadn't seemed openly nervous, but Nikki saw a line of sweat break out on his upper lip. "We don't perform on Mondays or Tuesdays."

He would have been free on the night of the murder. "Do you remember what you were doing this Tuesday evening?"

Perspiration covered his lips now, spreading to his cheeks and temples. He pulled out a red workman's handkerchief and mopped his face. "No, I can't. It's funny, it's only two nights ago and I don't seem—"

"That's okay, Mr. Maynard." She handed him her card. "If you think of it, give me a call." She stood up, followed him out. "Is that it on Matt Zaporelli?"

"Pretty much," he said.

They stopped near the lobby doors, where he seemed to remember something. "Wait a minute—there was more. The Zaporelli kid stole one of my pictures." He gestured toward the prints stapled to the walls. "That one." A bare spot showed on the brick, a rectangle bordered by staples. "It was a shot of Bernie and Zim, back when the theater started. The kid asked me did I have a picture of Zim, so I showed it to him. He almost jumped out of his skin. He asked could he have a copy, but it was the only one I had. When Bernie died six years ago I went through all his stuff. There weren't any pictures of Zim. Last month, when we put up this display, I found the picture stuck to the cover of one of the old boxes."

"You knew it was Zim?"

"It was signed. I remembered the police had been looking for a picture of him, so I copied it and sent it to Lawton. I figured it might help, even this late in the game. It wasn't a very good shot."

"Matt has the original?"

"He must have. We were out here talking, and the phone rang. I went to answer. When I came back he was gone and so was the picture."

"What did Zim look like? Anyone you recognized?"

He hesitated. "Not really."

"Thanks for your time."

Maynard pushed open the door. A soot-laden breeze filtered into the lobby. "If anything comes through on Bernie's murder, you'll let me know?"

"What makes you think there's a connection?"

He shrugged. "I keep hoping."

# 17

Nikki sensed something special going on the minute she reached the top of the station-house stairs. A crowd of detectives milled about expectantly, more than usual even allowing for the attention the case was getting. Smirks and leers, elbow nudgings. Jameson, who sat at the desk next to hers, cut his eyes toward the back, where the interrogation rooms were. "Oh mon," he said, "this case gets more and more interesting."

She dropped her purse into a drawer. "What's going on?"

"His Holiness had the Royce woman brought in." Even though Nikki was the primary detective, Eagle-Eye had ultimate responsibility for the case and could ask to have a suspect questioned if he thought it was necessary. Jameson winked. "A *big* improvement over the usual."

Nikki caught the aroma of garlic in the air and looked at him suspiciously. "What smells?"

He pulled a flat package from the depths of the kneehole. "*Cerdo asado*. Rodriguez's mother made it. The real thing, hot and spicy."

"One of these days they'll take you to Coney Island Hospital, pump you out."

"Ah, but think, mon, all the enjoyment I will have had getting there."

She got up to check her message slot and caught a glimpse of the silver-framed picture on her desk. She'd taken it last

Christmas. Dave and Lara, in matching aprons, stood behind the turkey they'd roasted. Dave's son and daughter had been with them that day—Scott, a senior at Pace; Tina, home for the holidays, in her second year at Yale. It had gone better than Nikki had hoped. Scott had been friendly, had asked Nikki about her cases, why she'd decided to become a cop.

For no apparent reason, she thought suddenly of her parents' hometown near Kavalla, on the rocky coast of Macedonia. There an unmarried woman of twenty-one was considered an old maid, her mother had told her. Nikki, her mother had pointed out, was ten years older than that, had turned thirty-one in February.

Cardone approached her. "I called the bus company," he said. A twenty-year veteran, Cardone was getting ready to retire this summer. "I talked to the dispatcher on that B thirty-one line, the Gerritsen bus." He mumbled when he talked to her but was clear otherwise. Nikki suspected he was uneasy working with a woman. He'd started speaking to her six months ago, after her first few clearances. Before that he'd acted as though she didn't exist. "This one guy's on that route at night, but he was out. I left the number."

"Thanks."

There was only one slip in her message slot. Stavich had called to let her know they were searching Zaporelli's Mercedes tomorrow at two. As primary investigator, she would be there, as she had been at the autopsy.

On her desk lay a printout from Federated National Savings Bank—activity on Zaporelli's account. The computer sheets went back twelve years, to the beginning of the account. Nikki found the most recent cash withdrawal, marked it with a red ballpoint star and worked backward to the earlier ones. Three thousand dollars, withdrawn like clockwork on the fourth Tuesday of every month. Elaine Lessing had been right on target.

Five, almost six years ago there had been a gap in the withdrawals. For three months there hadn't been any. Before that, they'd been only two thousand dollars. Quite a jump, two thousand to three thousand—what had happened? Had Karen moved to a fancier apartment? Why had there been a three-month gap? Out of curiosity, she turned to the beginning of the printout. No regular withdrawals. Zaporelli had started pulling out chunks of cash seven years ago, five years after he'd opened the account.

She strolled to the interrogation room. Doyle, a career detective with a good clearance record, stood outside peering through the one-way glass. Karen Royce, slim in a tailored skirt and belted sweater, sat in a chair, ankles trim, legs crossed. In a nervous gesture, she lifted the silky blond mass of hair from her shoulders, pushing it behind her ears. Her earrings and necklace looked like the real thing, not gold plated. Had they been gifts from Zaporelli?

"We're lettin' her cool," Doyle said. "Think things over."

"How's it going?" Nikki asked.

"I told her the doorman blew her alibi away, that she wasn't in bed like she said. So now her story is she was down in the dumps and went to the campaign office to booze away her troubles."

"She say why she lied?"

"She was ashamed of the drinking."

"My ten-year-old niece makes up better stories. Anyone see her there?"

"No, the place was closed. She was alone."

"So why'd she pull her car out at three thirty?" Nikki said. "To drive two blocks to the campaign office?"

"According to her, the garage guy made a mistake—lotsa people look like her, have the same car."

Karen had known Zaporelli's route—she could have driven out to Brooklyn, killed him near his mother's, then driven back home. If that had happened, it would change the picture into a domestic killing, almost as though they'd been spouses.

Nikki could picture Karen in a rage, putting a bullet through Zaporelli's head, another through the center of his pleasure. The gun fit, too. An automatic; some were small enough to slip into a purse, lightweight—a woman's gun. She made a mental note to have Karen's car checked for traces of blood or a recent cleanup job to erase them. What could have made her angry enough to kill?

"She says she came home at eight thirty, carrying some liquor," Doyle said. "The liquor store guy corrobs that—she bought some Scotch at eight fifteen."

"She a regular drinker?" Nikki asked.

"No—we checked around."

"She really got loaded—any idea why?"

"I asked her. She won't say."

Nikki said, "I need some time with her."

"She'll be here another half hour, at least." He scratched his crew cut. "By the way, His Holiness wants to see you." He jerked his thumb in the direction of Eagle-Eye's office. "He said for you to wait till he got back."

"When'll that be?"

"He didn't say."

"Know what he wants?"

"He said something about the Zaporelli kid."

She walked back to her desk. She wasn't any closer to finding Matt Zaporelli. She'd have nothing to tell Eagle-Eye. If he wasn't back by the time she finished questioning Karen Royce, she'd leave for her meeting with Dave and make up some excuse if he asked about it later. It was risky to disobey Eagle-Eye's orders. He had a certain amount of give, like a rubber band. If you went too far, he'd snap. She'd seen him discipline others but had so far managed to stay clear of his wrath.

She moved the bank records to one side and dialed information in Providence, Rhode Island. She reached the office of the dean of students at Brown University and discovered the dean was out. Nikki identified herself to an assistant and ex-

plained she wanted information on two students who'd been
at Brown a little more than twenty years ago, Bernard Chase
and Dean Zaporelli. Had they known one another, been connected in any way, been in any kind of trouble? The assistant
promised to tell the dean and have him return the call.

She typed a DD5 on the interview with Maynard, being careful in her choice of words, detailed in her explanations. In the
year she'd been a detective she'd learned to pay more attention
to the way she described things, to reread and sometimes re-
type whole pages. Reports were the part of her job she liked
least. When she was eighteen she'd spent a year as a secretary,
working for her cousin Achilles, the lawyer, and discovered she
hated typing. But she'd come to see that in detective work, reports really mattered. Paper was starting to pile up on the case.
It had overflowed a wire basket, begun to fill a carton next to it
marked with the case number and "ZAP."

The garlic smell was thicker. Jameson had unwrapped the
*cerdo asado* and laid it inside his top drawer. His phone rang.
"Detectives, Jameson speaking." He tore off a piece of pork,
swallowed it and registered shock at its spiciness. He fanned
his open mouth. "Wha's the address?" he asked, trying to talk
clearly around the mouthful.

Nikki picked up the bank printout and walked back to the
interrogation room. Two detectives watched Karen through
the one-way glass as Doyle questioned her. The first said,
"You think Zaporelli asked her to do something disgusting,
like some new position, and she got fed up and whacked him?"

"Maybe he started talking like you, dirtbag," the other answered, "and made her vomit."

Nikki waited till Doyle had finished. He passed Nikki on
the way out, shook his head. "Lotsa luck."

Recognition flashed in Karen's eyes as Nikki entered the
room, but she didn't say hello. "I came in willingly," she in-
formed Nikki. "I'd like to go home now."

"Sure." Nikki opened the printout and handed it to her.

"Just one thing—I thought you might be able to help with this. It's a record of activity on Mr. Zaporelli's bank account."

Almost imperceptibly, Karen's features tightened, became wary. She pushed her hair behind her ears. "What do you want to know?"

"See the entries next to the red stars? Mr. Zaporelli was taking three thousand dollars out of his account every month."

"So?" The corners of her mouth pinched, giving her face a worried look, making her beauty disappear for a moment.

"Rumor has it that money was used to pay your rent."

She stared for a moment as though Nikki had spoken in a foreign language. She said nothing, seemed to be thinking. Then, in a carefully controlled tone, "Who told you that?"

"Elaine Lessing."

She gave a short, mocking laugh. "I should've known. The walking gossip column. Anything you want to know. And if she doesn't know, she'll make it up, like this little tidbit." She recrossed her legs. "Elaine and I go way back—to Dean's law office."

"You worked together?"

She nodded, a wing of soft blond hair separating from the heavy mass and wafting with the motion. "She drove me nuts. Listened in on my calls, read my private mail. If I caught her, she'd apologize, but then she'd be back at it again. Like a little kid. I told Dean to get rid of her when he opened the campaign office. But she begged him for a job—any kind of job—and he felt sorry for her."

A lever tripped in Nikki's brain. Elaine had given a different version of events—that Zaporelli had offered *her* the job, had had to persuade her to take it. A minor point, but an inconsistency; she'd learned to pay attention to even the smallest inconsistency.

Karen said, "He hired her to keep an eye on Donna, who was becoming a pain. She fit right in, hovering over Donna—

Elaine never had a family of her own, so it suited her. She and Donna could sit and tell lies about me all day—that he was footing my rent, keeping me, that I was some kind of cheap prostitute being paid for sex."

Nikki thought for a moment, unsure how to phrase her next question. "He gave you gifts?" she finally said.

Her eyes darkened. "Sure. But I gave *him* things, too. I'm not poor. I have a trust fund my father left me. I don't *have* to work. I didn't even have a steady job till I met Dean." Her face reddened as though she were holding back tears.

"The three thousand wasn't for your rent?"

"Of course not."

"What *was* it for?"

"How should I know?"

She was hiding something. Nikki could tell from her sudden avoidance of eye contact, the quick lift of her head.

"You picked up the money at the bank, didn't you?"

"Yes, but I always gave it to him."

"And this Tuesday?"

"The same. He took it out to Brooklyn."

"How do you know?"

"He always—" She let the words hang as though she realized she'd said too much.

"He always took the money to Brooklyn—every month?"

"That's right."

"And what did he do with it?"

"I don't know." But she was looking at her lap, unable again to meet Nikki's glance.

"Miss Royce, Mr. Zaporelli had been taking this money out every month for—let's see—seven years. And you had no idea what it was for?"

Her fingers tightened on a tassel of the leather sack at her side. "No." Then, in a defensive tone, "He started the withdrawals seven years ago, right? Well, I only met him four years ago, when I went to work for him. This has nothing to do with me—he was taking that money out long before I ever laid eyes on him."

Yet she knew more than she was saying. Nikki sensed her discomfort; she'd put the sack on her lap and was looking at the door. "Miss Royce," Nikki said, "does the name Lantern Light Theater mean anything to you?"

"Yes." She seemed relieved that Nikki had changed the subject. "A man called the office. He said he was from there and asked for Dean."

"When was this?"

"About a week ago. His name was"—she looked off briefly—"Maynard. Peter Maynard."

"What happened?"

"Nothing. Dean wouldn't talk to him."

"Did he say why?"

"No. He didn't recognize Maynard's name or the name of the theater. He was busy—told me get rid of him. I had a lot of trouble getting this Maynard off the phone. He said if Dean wouldn't talk to him, he'd go see him. He said to ask Dean if the name Bernie Chase meant anything to him. I told Dean afterward but he just shrugged."

"He didn't say anything?"

"No." She rose, slung the bag over her shoulder. "Can I go?"

"Any time."

Nikki let her get as far as the doorway, then said, as though it were an afterthought. "By the way, I checked with Mr. Zaporelli's attorney—what his name—"

"McCander," Karen said.

"That's it. He said he wasn't aware that Mr. Zaporelli had any intention of divorcing his wife. Could Mr. Zaporelli have used another lawyer?"

Karen's mouth thinned and tightened. "I said he was *planning* to see an attorney."

"I could've sworn you'd said he *had* seen one."

Nikki guessed if Karen had had a gun in her bag she'd have shot Nikki right then, without regret. "No. I said he was going to. Right after the election." She spun on her heel and left without another word.

# 18

Nikki waited in the Yemeni Restaurant, watching the brocade draperies sway lazily under the ceiling fan, listening to songs plucked on the *qanun*, which sounded like the Greek bouzouki. The sticky-sweet aroma of baking apricots rose in her nostrils.

She should never have agreed to meet Dave here.

She pulled out her hand mirror, checked her eye makeup, scratched at a tiny dark speck on her eyelid. She hated putting on mascara, always managed to jam the brush into her eye or land the stuff on her lids. Why had she bothered with it? She'd stuck it on, had also taken time to change from tailored pumps to sandals, from silver button earrings to the gold pendants Dave had given her on her last birthday.

At five forty he walked into the dining room and followed the maitre d' to her table. He wore a dark striped shirt that intensified his deep coloring, making him look like a Mafia prince. For a moment her heart forgot how to beat. She turned away so he wouldn't see the expression in her eyes.

"Sorry I'm late." He carried a portfolio and slid it next to him on the banquette. He didn't lean over to kiss her hello, their usual greeting. She realized he was wearing a new sports jacket, new to her at least. She thought she knew all his clothes. Had he just bought it? She didn't remember his mentioning it. A sudden thought occurred to her—was he simply refurbishing his wardrobe or outfitting himself for a fuller social life, getting ready to go out more. On dates, maybe. After all, she had no claim on him—was that what he'd been trying to tell her this morning in Zaporelli's lobby?

"The stiff in the subway turns out to be a Jane Doe, no ID, nothing," he said. "Just twenty-three stab wounds in her back." She tried not to stare at his eyes, the sprinkling of black bits near the center of his irises, made an effort to focus on what he was saying. "She was homeless?"

"Looked like it. Had a regular spot on this subway bench, had been there every night for almost a month. Took a while for the morgue guys to come." The maitre d' hovered near their table. "You order?" Dave asked.

"Not yet." She always started with laban, Arabic-style yogurt with cucumbers, while he had the homus, minced chickpeas. They'd put both plates between them and share. She waited for him to tell the maitre d', "We'll have the usual," but instead he asked for menus. A small thing, but it threw her off.

He studied the gold-tasseled carte, then said to the maitre d', "Chicken concasseli and some white zinfandel."

"No appetizer today, sir?"

"No."

"And what will madame have?"

She said, "I don't know." Dave wasn't going to share an appetizer tonight. Or, she realized with sudden awareness, much of anything else that was personal. Was she magnifying a small difference into a whole new attitude on his part? She felt uncertain, as though she didn't really know him. For all their intimacy over the past year, tonight he seemed like a stranger. The maitre d' cleared his throat, jarring her out of her thoughts. "The chicken too," she said lamely.

Dave opened the portfolio as soon as the maitre d' left. He pulled out a sheaf of papers and some photographs. "The Nose Job—Bernie Chase." He handed her the prints.

They were crime-scene shots. A man, clothed in a bloodied shirt and trousers, lay on his back near a bed, hands reaching futilely over his head, groping for something he would never touch. She remembered the genial-looking man in the photo above Peter Maynard's desk but found it hard to connect this picture with Chase. A patch of the fair hair was visible, squashed behind his ear. A dark, irregular shape on the carpet around his torso marked the flow of blood and life from his body. "He was in a motel," Dave said, "the Modern—that big place on the Belt. According to the M.E. he got it in the chest and gut. In bed probably, from the amount of blood on the sheets. He managed to crawl or fall onto the carpet—tried to reach the phone from the way his arms look, never made it. And after he was gone, the perp rearranged his face a little, put a big hole where his nose should've been."

Under the first photo was a close-up of the face. "Oh God!" she said.

"Yeah. He wasn't pretty."

The zinfandel arrived. The *qanun* was playing mournfully now, a sorrowful melody that reminded Nikki of her grandmother's ironing songs. Her grandmother would press the family's clothing, singing for hours—old Greek tunes about lovers who were far apart, lost loves. *Min akous ton patera sou, tha eimaste panta mazi*, "Don't listen to your father—we belong together."

Dave poured some of the pale wine into each of their glasses. Out of habit she waited for him to toast—lift his glass and say, "Here's to you, Stretch." Or if he were feeling romantic, "To my fair lady." But tonight he sipped his wine without a word. She did the same, fighting the disappointment she felt. She became aware of an unfocused anger; she could be eating with Stavich or Jameson—any cop, for that matter. She couldn't pinpoint why she was angry or with whom, but she was so unsettled that for a brief moment her mind rebelled and refused to think about Zaporelli or Chase. She couldn't even remember why she'd asked for this meeting. Then she forced herself back to the file.

She pointed to the close-up. "That extra shot—that's *my* killer's M.O. What kind of gun?"

"An automatic. A Walther."

She felt excitement stir. "That connects, too." She leafed through the pile of reports and found the ballistics rundown. "I'm going to take this to the lab, have them compare Zaporelli's slugs."

He dipped a piece of pita into the concasseli sauce. "We could never make a case, didn't even have a suspect. It looked drug-related. When they found him, there was a fresh bag of coke on the dresser, not even opened."

"He'd just made a buy?"

"That's what it looked like. His kind doesn't wait once they have the stuff. A recreational user, but in a big way. A gram a week habit."

"No one heard the shots?"

"The radio was loud, and there was only one other room rented on that floor, way at the other end. Chase had checked in about an hour before—"

"He didn't live there?"

"No. He was living at this theater he ran, the Lantern Light."

"So why did he take the motel room?"

He put down his zinfandel and leaned toward her, one eyebrow raised in the characteristic triangular peak that had always fascinated her. "Now *that* is the sixty-four-thousand-dollar question."

"To meet someone, maybe."

"And whoever he met snuffed him. I had a thought—he might have arranged for a drug delivery, and if he owed the dealer big bucks—But that didn't go anywhere. We could never figure out who was supplying him." He tore a piece of steaming pita and dabbed butter inside its fold. "We looked for a love interest—he dated women from time to time. But there was no one steady, not even recent. The guy lived for the theater. He'd been working down on Wall Street for years, an accounting job for the Exchange, running the theater at night."

"When did he sleep?"

"After the place closed. About four, five hours a night. A year before he died, he came into some money, quit the day job and worked the theater full time. Hired an assistant—"

"Peter Maynard. I met him."

"Yeah?" His eyebrow peaked again.

"Looking for Zaporelli's son."

"Oh. Well, Maynard's still hot on the case," Dave said. "It's six years, and the guy keeps coming up with new leads, won't let it rest. Like he lost his father. Latest thing, he heard from a P.I. in Brooklyn, a guy named Bienstock, who's supposed to have something good. Would I check it out."

"He showed me Bienstock's card. Did you go out there?"

"Not yet."

She leafed through the other photos, shots of the bed, the unopened cocaine, the bedroom floor. Dave said, "Case was a stinker. No one knew anything, saw anything. The desk clerk at the motel didn't remember anyone asking for Chase, but there're a million ways to get into a big place like the Modern—side door, back, garage."

"Someone came in, took care of him, slipped out."

"A real clever someone. Neat and careful."

She frowned. "Zaporelli's killer tidied up, picked up both shells."

He tapped the photo with a blunt finger. "So did this perp. No prints or cigarette butts, nothing we could use."

She felt her excitement grow, as though she'd sighted the killer—a distant, blurred view, but still a glimpse. A shadowy figure in a crime scene, carefully removing anything incriminating.

She took a bite of the chicken but found she had no appetite. She put down her fork.

"What's wrong?"

"I shouldn't have ordered all this," she said.

"It's the case, isn't it?"

She nodded. "I want to get over to Ballistics."

"I'll go with you. If anything connects, it'll be the biggest break I've had so far on Chase."

She'd wanted him to go with her. But not because he needed to clear up an open file. Didn't he want to be with her? She remembered then that *she* was the one who had asked for space, had pushed him away. But she hadn't realized how much she'd miss the warm, tender side of him. What was *wrong* with her? Was she never satisfied? She suddenly thought of what her life had been like before she'd met him— she'd had Lara and her work. But somehow she pictured that time as a desert, a dry landscape she'd walked across each day, alone.

"The Chase slugs should still be down at Ballistics," he said. He signaled for the check.

# 19

Traffic was unexpectedly heavy on the Brooklyn–Queens Expressway as they headed toward the Ballistics lab in Manhattan. Dave drove, leaving Nikki free to look through material in the Chase file, between them.

"Ballistics better come up with something good," she said, "or I may be off the case. My boss thinks I'm wasting time, that the two cases don't connect. Plus he's pissed at me. I was supposed to sit at the station and wait for him—instead I came out to meet you."

"He'd take you off the case?"

"Better believe it. Dritzer didn't want me on to begin with."

"You think the two cases connect?" Dave asked.

"They have to. Maynard called Zaporelli—Zaporelli's girlfriend told me. Said he had information that would interest Zaporelli, mentioned Chase's name."

"What did he have?"

"I don't know. Maynard says he didn't know Zaporelli." Across the water the lights of Manhattan's financial district dotted the evening sky, a glowing geometric pattern on a giant screen. "The other thing is Zaporelli's son, Matt. Matt went down to the theater, saw a picture of Chase and his partner, Zim, and was excited enough to lift it off the wall."

"This one?" He steered with one hand, used the other to grope under the papers. He handed her a black-and-white enlargement. A double portrait showed two men in their late twenties standing before a theater curtain and smiling at the camera, arms around one another in a comradely fashion.

She recognized Chase from the picture in Maynard's office. The other man was dark and lean. Both had signed the picture. The dark man's signature was heavy and bold, with a backward tilt: "Tony Zim." He wore a gaucho costume, a bolero and some kind of wide-brimmed hat that threw his face into shadow. A narrow mustache trimmed his lip. The photo had been taken onstage, with insufficient light, and had a grainy, unclear quality.

She had a sudden thought—if Matt had stolen the original of this photo from the Lantern Light, he would have taken it home and shown it to his roommate, Glenn. Glenn might know what the significance of the picture was.

Dave tapped Zim's face. "This is the only picture of Zim we have. It's not great, but at least it's something. There was no trace of the guy."

"There should have been?"

"You bet. He was in almost every production the theater ran. He and Chase were very tight at one time, and then there was some kind of fight and he split. There should have been *something*. It was like he never existed outside of his signature on checks, his name in the early programs."

"What about the other actors, couldn't they give you a lead?"

"There wasn't much of a company. Chase couldn't afford to pay. People would drift in, act in one or two shows, move on. There was one woman who played opposite Zim for a while, but she'd died the year before Chase was killed."

They left the Brooklyn Bridge, passed One Police Plaza, the dull brown building that housed the Commissioner's office and was nerve center for the whole NYPD. "I ran my butt off looking for Zim," Dave said. "He was the only live lead we had. Chase was harmless. He didn't have an enemy in the world. His only trouble had happened years before, when this girl died, a young actress connected with the theater."

"The garbage-bag case?"

"Yeah. Lisa Hirsch. She wasn't *in* a garbage bag. She was on a pile of them in an alley a couple of blocks from the theater. An accidental death, a drug overdose. Anyhow, right after that, Zim splits. Leaves the theater and goes up in smoke.

"You mentioned Chase suddenly came into some money— where'd it come from?"

"No idea. There was no record of anything. But he had enough money to give up the job and work in the theater full time."

"When did this happen, the money thing?"

"I know what you're thinking," Dave said. "That Zim paid Chase to keep him undercover after the Hirsch girl's death. No good. Chase didn't come into his money till five years after Zim disappeared. He didn't quit his job till then."

The Ballistics lab was housed in a room on the eighth floor of the Police Academy building. The "mike" room, where microscope comparisons were made, looked like a small lab, with scientific instruments and equipment. Matchless Marvin Grant peered through his eyepiece at both slugs, the one that had been in Zaporelli's groin and the one that had killed Chase. He slowly turned each in the positioning clay, lined up the rifling in the viewer. "They're both right sixes," he said.

He slid off his stool and faced Nikki. He was a tall, shapeless man, hunched from years of bending over a microscope. "Want my opinion? Same gun."

Nikki felt her excitement rise.

She and Dave walked to the hallway and waited for the elevator. "I'd better let Eagle-Eye know," she said. "I have to call Lara, too—she should be home by now."

She found a pay phone in the lobby, waited for a blue-suited cadet to finish his call. The lab was in the Police Academy building, where she'd spent months jumping hurdles, physical and mental, toughening herself so she could join the force, eager to put on the blue uniform.

She called home first. "Where are you?" Lara asked. She sounded lonely.

"In the city." Nikki added impulsively, "With Uncle Dave."

"Good!"

"Lara!"

Dave, standing nearby, looked up at her sharp tone. She lowered her voice. "We're working on a case."

"Oh." Her voice fell. "When'll you be home?"

"Late, probably. If I'm not there to say good night, I'll see you in the morning."

"Okay." For months and months it *had* been okay. Tonight Lara sounded unhappy. She didn't see enough of Nikki. But if Nikki married, Lara would have to share her. She doubted Lara had figured that out. Otherwise she wouldn't be pushing Nikki so eagerly to the altar. She suddenly felt sorry for her, for all the times she couldn't be there for her. "Look, I'll make it up to you, okay? Two stories tomorrow instead of one. What're we up to?"

"Hercules and the Twelve Labors. What if you don't come home early tomorrow?"

"Then I'll owe you three stories. One a night. Deal?"

"Deal."

"I love you, Lara."

"I love you too."

She dialed the precinct and got through to Eagle-Eye. "Ah, Trakos," he said, his voice filled with false delight. "A pleasure to hear from you. Thanks so much for waiting for me earlier."

"I got a lead to the Zaporelli boy," she said. "A cabbie sighted him, so I ran out to question the guy. But it was a false alarm."

She could tell from the long silence he didn't believe her. "Where the fuck are you?"

"Down at Ballistics."

"What in hell are you doing down there?"

She explained the new developments.

"How'd Lawton get into this? Ya told me ya didn't wanna work with him."

"Stavich called him," she lied. An image flashed through her mind, Father Ephraem, the old priest at St. Spyridon's, who'd frightened her as a child towering over her in his black vestments and hat; *Lying is a mortal sin*, he'd said. "Stavich told Lawton about Zaporelli and he thought there might be a connection."

"What kinda connection?"

She went through it again, and then a third time. She could tell he was still confused when she finished. "Dritzer called," he said. "He's fuckin' unhappy. I gotta give him more than promises."

"It's shaping up," she said, wishing that were true. She couldn't tell him how confused she felt, how none of the facts she'd collected so far seemed to tell any kind of story.

"Where're you headed?" he asked irritably.

"To see a private eye named Bienstock."

"*Who the fuck is he?*"

"I'll explain when I get back."

"Listen, Trakos—"

A recorded voice asked for more money to continue the conversation. "I don't have another quarter," she said. She heard him shout "Trakos!" once, then she hung up.

"Let's get out of here," she said to Dave.

# 20

East New York, once a middle-class neighborhood of densely populated apartment buildings and two-family houses, had slipped into a high-crime, low-income ghetto. Reuben Bienstock, P.I., lived on Georgia Avenue, near the corner of Riverdale, in the basement apartment of a brick row house. On the upper floor one window was covered with plywood. In another a torn shade hung at an angle.

Nikki and Dave pulled up near a pile of uncollected garbage against which a dog urinated. A crowd of teenagers on the corner eyed Dave's Chevy.

"Be lucky to have a car when I get out," he said to Nikki.

A gangly, dark-skinned boy with a shaved head and a bouncy gait detached himself from the crowd. He wore a zipper jacket with a dragon appliquéd under the pocket. "Hey man, watch your car?"

"Sure." Dave pulled out a dollar. "That's a deposit. If it's all there when I come out, you get more."

"O-*kay!*"

Bienstock answered the door dressed in a grimy T-shirt, a soiled white blazer and checked slacks. He was grossly overweight, shapeless, as though someone had pumped air into his frame and inflated it to twice the ordinary size. An inch of gray hair circled his skull like a fringe. He welcomed them genially, even after they'd shown their badges. "Come in, come in. *Two* officers! Well, I *am* fortunate tonight." He spoke with a British accent.

The smell of ammonia hit Nikki as she entered, burning her eyes. A white-and-black cat with a mustache-like patch under its nose slid past, and she realized what she was smelling was cat urine. Specks of dry cat food littered the lumpy sofa; open cans covered the tops of the filing cabinets that crowded every corner. Nikki counted fourteen cabinets, some single and some two-drawer, battered veterans that had to have come from garbage dumps or off the street.

"Sit down, won't you?"

She walked past the uninviting sofa and settled herself gingerly on a wooden chair. Dave took another.

"I would offer you something," Bienstock said, "a cup of tea, perhaps? But it seems I'm fresh out of tea." He laughed, though Nikki couldn't see the humor in what he'd said.

He seated himself, melting across the center pillow of the sofa. The mustached cat sprang up and lay across his midsection. He stroked it, the animal diminished by his massive hands.

Nikki said, "I understand we have a mutual acquaintance, Mr. Bienstock. Peter Maynard."

Nikki saw the slight narrowing of his eyes as he registered the name, but he said, "Maynard? I'm not sure I—"

"The Lantern Light Theater—does that help your memory?"

"Oh yes, of course. The Hirsch girl."

She wondered where Bienstock was taking her—it was Chase she'd come to talk about. "Did you ever meet Maynard?" she asked.

"I may have." Bienstock laid the cat on the floor. "Everything is so dear these days—inflation is the problem, I believe. When I was younger and in demand I could afford to be generous, but now, you see, I'm old, trying to get by on Social Security and whatever small sums I can pick up."

Dave laid a twenty on the coffee table. Bienstock gave the

bill an amused, contemptuous look. A long minute passed. Nikki pulled a second twenty from her purse and covered Dave's with it. Bienstock leaned down and stroked the cat, who rubbed back and forth against his legs. "An old man, Saddam, that's what I've become. Struggling to stay alive in an unfriendly world."

Dave stood, scooped the twenties off the table, said, "Come on," to Nikki.

They'd crossed halfway to the door when Bienstock sang out, "My goodness, such impatience!" He rushed past them, surprisingly swift for a man of his bulk, and blocked their escape. He pulled the twenties from Dave's hand. "No need to rush off like that."

They took their seats in the living room again. Bienstock panted from the effort of his run. He put the forty back on the table. Nikki felt as though he were stage-managing the scene. He knew exactly how far to push them and had decided long before they came just how much he would say.

"You were telling us about Maynard," she said.

Bienstock sighed. "I was hired six years ago by a woman named Rose Hirsch to look into the death of her daughter, Lisa. The police had called it accidental—a drug overdose—and she didn't believe it. She thought her daughter had been killed. She wanted to know who had done it, and why."

"Was she right? Had the girl been killed?"

He stooped to pick up the cat. Nikki had the feeling he was trying to avoid eye contact. "I could never find out. She was a wild girl, very beautiful. The mother had been raising her alone; the father had deserted. She was the passion of her mother's life, and she was stagestruck. One day she moved out of her mother's house and went to live at an off-off-Broadway theater. She wouldn't tell the mother where."

"The Lantern Light?"

"As it turns out. And she got into trouble."

"What kind of trouble?"

He bent to drop the cat onto the floor. His eyes were hidden again. "I never found out."

Dave said, "If that's all you produced for the mother, I'd say you weren't worth shit."

Bienstock raised his head as though he'd been struck. A deep laugh started in his belly and rolled into the room. "My, my. A very outspoken young man."

"Maynard told me you had something hot on the Chase murder," Nikki said. "What was it?"

"Did he tell you that? I don't recall saying it."

Dave leaned back in disgust. Nikki knew from past investigations that his disgust wasn't real; he was being the "tough" cop, leaving the friendlier role to her. "Mr. Bienstock," she said, "you probably heard about Dean Zaporelli's murder."

"Yes, a shame, a good man."

"It's my feeling he was involved with the Lantern Light in some way."

"Interesting." His eyebrow lifted, yet she had the feeling she wasn't telling him anything new. "His son came to see me."

"Matt?"

"I believe that was the feller's name. Sad young chap. Looked like he needed a keeper. I couldn't spend much time with him. He didn't have the wherewithal to obtain the answers to his questions—if you follow me." Again the low laugh, more like a rumble than a chuckle.

"When was he here?"

"A week ago."

"What did he want?"

"He asked if I had pictures of some of the performers at the Lantern Light."

"Tony Zim?"

"I believe he mentioned that name."

"And do you?"

The briefest hesitation. "No."

Dave stood up, flexed his shoulders. "Want to know what I

think? You're full of shit!" He took a step toward Bienstock. Nikki thought he would pick up the money and go into his let's-get-out-of-here routine again but he didn't. "You got pictures here somewhere, old man. In one of these fucking file cabinets."

He and Bienstock had a ten-second staring contest before the rumbling chuckle started in the old man's throat. "You are persistent, sir. I'll grant you that."

He hoisted himself to his feet, waddled to a scratched red cabinet in the corner, and tugged out the bottom drawer. He pulled out an eight-by-ten print, handed it to Nikki. "Lisa Hirsch."

She *had* been beautiful. Winged eyebrows over merry dark eyes, a gaminlike face, soft cascade of brown curls.

"What do you have on Chase?" Dave said. "Cut the bullshit, Bienstock, or I'll run you in to the station, you can do your act down there."

A ten-second pause, then "My, my, my!" He stooped over the red filing cabinet, his rear end surprisingly small, lost in the wrinkles of his pants. "Will this help you? A photo of the chap." He handed Nikki a print of the double portrait of Chase and Zim.

"Thought you said you didn't have any pictures of Zim," Dave said.

Bienstock tilted his head, the fat on his neck jiggling. "Why, so I did!"

Dave took a step toward the door. "Let's go."

Nikki felt something stuck to the back of the print. She turned it over and found an address taped to it. "Bernard Chase, 2493 Plumb 2nd Street, Brooklyn, NY."

It took a few seconds to make the connection, to remember where she'd seen the address before. The Chaikins lived there. Celia Chaikin had found Zaporelli's body while walking her dog.

# 21

"Sol Chaikin is Chase's brother," Dave told her as they drove along the Belt parkway. The water in Jamaica Bay churned up in whitecaps. A tattered newspaper blew across the scrub grass, joined a pile of litter under a bush. Dave rummaged through the papers on the seat, found a DD5 completed six years earlier and held it against the steering wheel. "Sol and Celia Chaikin. Little nebbish guy with a battleship wife?"

"That's them."

"I did the interview myself. Chase changed his name when he was sixteen, seventeen." He scanned the report. "Chaikin and the wife said they hadn't had contact with Chase for years."

"Zaporelli's murder puts a different twist on things."

"You run a check on them?" he asked.

"Yes. Neither one has a sheet."

He stopped at a phone stand on Flatbush Avenue, called the homicide office, huddled against the stand to block the wind. He came back to the car and slid behind the wheel. "You know that Jane Doe I picked up in the subway?"

"The homeless woman?"

"I *thought* she was homeless. Put her through missing persons and we got a call. Man in Boston wants to come take a look. I have to get over there." That didn't sound like a date, she comforted herself. At least he'd explained.

He left her at the station house. She'd decided it was time

to come into the precinct, face Eagle-Eye's anger, and explain to him where the case was going. But Eagle-Eye wasn't there.

"He went out for an hour," Stavich told her. Stavich was using her typewriter, hunched over, his shoulders rounded with exhaustion as he pecked at the keys. A borrowed ashtray on her desk held a pyramid of butts; the air was stale with smoke. "He's pissed at you."

Nikki'd been counting on Eagle-Eye to be there so she could calm him down. She'd hoped that by now she'd have something concrete to present to him, to justify the time she'd spent. But all she had were suspicions, leads that went nowhere. It wasn't good enough, not now when he was trying to convince Dritzer to keep her on as case detective. For the first time she wondered how long Dritzer would let her stay, when the breaking point would come.

"Whadya tell him," Stavich said, "that I called Lawton to ask about the Nose-Job case?"

"I never said that. He gets things screwed up."

Stavich frowned. His small eyes seemed to disappear completely. "He's boiled on accounta you didn't stay till he got back this afternoon."

"I had an appointment to get my legs waxed." Stavich stared at her blankly. He was taking her seriously. She wondered whether she should explain the sarcasm, gave up and asked, "How're you making out with the Zaporelli kid?"

"Nowhere and nothing. Spent the whole damned day trailing the roommate around again."

"Taylor?"

"Yeah. He's gonna make an appeal on the ten o'clock news." He checked his watch. "Any minute now."

Nikki followed him to the TV, where two detectives sprawled in front of a rerun of *Shane*. Stavich changed the channel. "Sorry guys—duty calls. Just be a minute."

"Hey, shithead, put the movie back on," the first said.

"Duty *balls*," the second complained.

Matt's disappearance was the lead story. A tearful Glenn spoke about his concern for his roommate. He looked haggard. The camera emphasized deep hollows in his cheeks, darkened the stubble on his jaw. "If you have any information," Glenn pleaded in a shaky voice, "call the police hot-line number. Matt, if you're out there and you're watching, just let me know you're okay. *Please*."

Watching the appeal, Nikki remembered she'd wanted to question Glenn about the picture Matt had taken from the Lantern Light. Had Matt talked to him about it?

"It don't look good," Stavich said as they walked back to Nikki's desk. "The kid ain't been seen in a coupla days."

Nikki said, "I had two leads on him, but they were earlier in the week." She explained Matt had gone to see Maynard at the Lantern Light, then talked to Bienstock.

"Why'd he go there?"

"He was trying to get something on his father—Zaporelli controlled an inheritance of his. He wouldn't give him a cent till he shaped up."

"You think he whacked his old man?" Stavich asked.

"Maybe, maybe not. But I've been thinking—the dirt he collected on his father might put him in danger."

"How?"

"From whoever *did*."

He stubbed out his cigarette, pulled on his coat. "I'm goin' back downtown. The roommate may get something from that TV spot—the kid may call."

If he's alive, Nikki thought.

A stocky, dark man in a bus driver's uniform approached them. "Detective Trakos?"

"I'm Detective Trakos."

"I just come off duty—I drive that B thirty-one bus, goes down Gerritsen. I was on the night Zaporelli got killed. I been reading about it in the papers, how it was so close to the route. I never picked no one up that night."

The canvass of taxi companies had yielded nothing. Nikki suddenly realized why she wasn't surprised. A killer as careful as this one would have hesitated to take a taxi. Taxi records could be checked.

If the killer hadn't hailed a cab, that left only public transportation or a second car. "You're sure no one got on at that corner—or even two or three blocks away?"

"I'd know. At that hour I ride for blocks before I get a passenger. I mean I got my regulars, people I know. It ain't like Avenue U, where a whole crowd gets on and you can't see who's who. I go past most stops with no pickup, so I'd remember. Nothin' that night."

He was almost at the door when he looked back. "If it was me, and I wanted to disappear, Avenue U is where *I'd* go. It's only seven blocks away. The U bus connects to the subway, and you can go anywhere you want."

"That's pretty good. Ever think of taking the police exam?"

He grinned. "No, thanks."

She thought about what he'd said after he left. It made sense for the perp to ride on a more populated line so he wouldn't be noticed. Assuming that's what the killer had done, had he known about both bus lines or just walked blindly, trying to stay out of sight? Or was she way off altogether, dealing with a perp who'd had his own car at the scene?

Jameson came in and threaded his way through the desks, his face drawn, gray under his coffee-toned skin.

"You okay?" Nikki asked.

"A little rocky."

"Something you ate?"

He glared at her, his usual good humor gone.

She checked her message slips. Fishberg, Donna's doctor, had phoned in. She dialed, reached his service, gave her name and number.

The dean at Brown, Dr. Praschkauer, had left his home number. He picked up on the fourth ring. "Praschkauer speaking."

Nikki thanked him for his earlier call.

"Happy to help. I took the records home thinking you might phone. Let's see—you wanted information on Bernard Chase and Dino Zaporelli. They did indeed attend at the same time. In fact they were good friends before they came. On their applications both asked if they could share a room."

"Any problems with either one?"

"Chase was suspended for drug use at one point, but he gave it up. At any rate he convinced the board he'd given it up, made up his credits, and was allowed to graduate with his class. He received an award for his participation in Sock and Buskin, our drama group. He was student director. That was his major—dramatic arts."

"And Zaporelli?"

"Pre-law, though he did act in the drama group. A fair-to-middling student. Nothing spectacular."

Nikki thanked him and put down the phone. Zaporelli and Chase—close friends before college, roommates while they were there. And afterward? She thought back to the photo of Chase and his partner, Tony Zim, remembered that Mark Zaporelli had become excited when he'd seen it. She was sure she understood why—Mark had recognized his father; Zaporelli had acted in Bernie Chase's theater after school, using the name Tony Zim.

The phone rang. It was Donna's doctor, Leon Fishberg.

"I have some questions on Donna Zaporelli," Nikki said. "I was wondering whether—"

"I did this already." His tone was clipped, as though he turned off his bedside manner when he left his patients. "I talked to a detective this morning."

"I know; I saw the report. But I have some questions of my own." She waited for an answer, became aware of Jameson sipping ginger ale at the next desk, Eagle-Eye's private line ringing in his office. There was so long a silence Nikki wondered whether he was still on the line. "Dr. Fishberg?"

"I'm still here. What do you want to know?"

"I don't understand rheumatoid arthritis that well. What kind of muscle strength does Mrs. Zaporelli have? For instance, could she—" She tried to think of an activity that required the same exertion as firing a weapon, couldn't, and in the end simply said, "Could she fire a gun?"

"A gun?" He sounded outraged. "What're you trying to do? Donna Zaporelli is one of the sweetest, gentlest women I know. She—"

"Dr. Fishberg, I *have* to ask these questions. Would she be able to?"

"Well, it depends. Some days yes and others no. She's affected by everything—chemical balances, mood, even weather. That's why I suggested Sunnycrest to Mr. Zaporelli, because of the drier climate."

"Sunnycrest?"

Another long pause. "Look," he said, "I don't mind answering questions about her physical condition, but when you ask me anything else you're on private family territory. I don't know that I'd have to answer, not even in a court of law. If that's it—"

Nikki started to say she had no more questions, heard a click, then a dial tone, and realized he'd hung up. Mr. Civility—or should that be *Doctor* Civility?

She scribbled the name Sunnycrest on her blotter, dialed Donna's number. No one answered. When the machine came on, she left her name and number, hung up.

A drier climate. That suggested Arizona. She tried information. There was no Sunnycrest in Arizona. Nevada and New Mexico didn't have one either.

She thought back to her conversation with Fishberg. He'd been even-tempered when they talked about Donna's condition, had mentioned Sunnycrest casually, as a suggestion of his—"a drier climate would help." It was only when she'd picked up on the name, asked about it, that he'd become hostile. "Private family territory." No trespassing.

She called information again and asked for the number of

Dr. George Akalaides, her parents' family doctor. It suddenly occurred to her that if Akalaides were still alive, he might not be practicing anymore—he must be almost her father's age, and her father was nearing eighty. The operator said, "One moment, please," then gave her the number. She dialed and heard his answering device. The message had been recorded in Dr. Akalaides's own voice, his thick Greek accent. It took Nikki back twenty years, made her feel Lara's age again. She remembered one visit when she'd revealed her mortification that she was taller than all the boys in her class. She'd asked the doctor tearfully when she would stop growing. He'd smiled and explained that only God knew, that He had decided that even before she was born. Now she left her name and number on the machine, asked for a return call.

In the middle of her desk lay the report on Karen Royce's car. It had been checked for bloodstains and gunpowder residue and showed neither. It hadn't been recently washed.

The long black hand on the clock jumped from second to second. Ten forty.

She should call the Chaikins, let them know she was coming over—it was getting late. But before she did, she wanted to start a credit check on them. She'd need a signed subpoena for that. She couldn't take the time to get the D.A.'s signature now. "How busy are you?" she asked Jameson.

"Why?" His skin was coming back to its normal color. A row of empty ginger-ale cans marched across his desk. He opened a fresh one, tipped it back for a long swallow. "What do you need?"

"The D.A.'s signature on a subpoena."

"Well, I don't know—" He looked at her slyly. "Remember you were telling me your aunt makes these grape leaf things with meat inside?"

"*Dolmades*? How can you even *think* about food right now? I was going to call EMS before, get an ambulance for you."

"A few of those *dolmades* things would be wonderful, Trakos."

She shrugged. "If that's what you want—"

"How would you like this subpoena filled out?"

At ten forty-five she dialed the Chaikins' number. A sleepy Sol Chaikin said, "*Hul*-lo."

"This is Detective Trakos."

A quick intake of breath on the other end. "Oh."

"I have to talk to you again. Mrs. Chaikin there?"

"Yeah." He breathed heavily into the receiver. "It's late. Do you know what time—"

"It's important, Mr. Chaikin."

"Why can't you do your work during the day, like the rest of the world?"

In the background she heard Celia's voice. "Who is it?" Then a muffled sound, as if someone had covered the phone with a hand. Snatches of conversation, not fully audible.

The next voice Nikki heard was Celia's. "When?" she said. "When will you come?"

Nikki had promised to call Dave and give him time to meet her so they could do the interview together. "In the next hour."

"Okay. We'll be ready."

# 22

The shepherds and shepherdesses lolled on their ceramic mounds, locked inside the Chaikins' display cases. Celia sat near the fireplace, zipped into a silver brocade dressing robe that looked like armor, the poodle next to her. Pippi's ribbons were silver tonight too—did Celia change them to match her outfits?

Sol was openly nervous. He slouched in an armchair and tugged at the belt of his silk lounge jacket, playing with its fringes. He resembled his brother—had the same soft features and uncertain look Bernie Chase had had; that was why Chase's photo had looked familiar, Nikki realized. Next to Sol, on an antique table, stood a framed photo of a young soldier holding a pistol, his legs apart in firing position. With a jolt, Nikki recognized the man—it was Sol, thirty years ago, slim and competent-looking, showing off his marksman's stance.

"Mr. Chaikin, how well did you know Dean Zaporelli?" she asked. She sat near the marble mantel, where plump angels flew toward each other, fingers not quite touching. She'd sunk deep into a plush chair; the muzzle of her .38 dug into her hip.

"I didn't know him," Sol said.

"He was your brother's best friend."

"So? That doesn't mean I knew him." He took a handkerchief out of his pocket, mopped his face. Dave had been listening, at the same time looking around at the pickled oak

floors and softly polished furniture. He threw her a disbelieving look.

"Mr. Chaikin," she said, "the dean at Brown told me your
brother and Mr. Zaporelli were close friends *before* they came
to school. They asked to share a room and—"

"That doesn't mean I knew the man." His voice had risen.
"I was nine years older than Bernie. We lived in different
worlds."

"So Mr. Zaporelli just decided that five blocks from here
was the perfect place to get killed?"

"How do I know! He could have!" His eyes pleaded with
Celia to rescue him.

Her features were masklike under her makeup, her hair a
helmet of copper. She said, "Stranger things have happened."

Sol sat up suddenly and pointed at Dave. "I remember! You
were the detective on Bernie's case—you came here once."

"Six years ago," Dave said.

Sol pressed his lips together. "They never did find out who
killed Bernie." He tugged his belt tighter around his waist. "I
knew he was going to end up in trouble. He was the bright one
in the family, right? The talented one. Look where it got him."

Nikki said, "It turns out your brother and Zaporelli were
killed with the same gun." She watched Sol carefully, but the
only reaction she saw was puzzlement, as though he couldn't
absorb the information.

"Maybe they'll get somewhere on Bernie's murder now," he
said. "I'll tell you the same thing I told your buddy six years
ago: I didn't know his friends, he didn't know mine. I was out
working before he even got out of public school."

It was plausible. Why didn't she believe him?

Dave broke in. "What do you do, Mr. Chaikin? Refresh me."

"I'm retired now—I was a math teacher."

"That's right." Dave's glance traveled around the room
again. Nikki sensed the question behind his eyes—how could
the Chaikins afford their luxuries on a teacher's salary? Had

Celia worked too? Maybe they had no children; she thought of the constant drain on her own salary because of Lara—clothing, dental bills, school supplies.

She asked Celia, who sat near her on the sofa, "Your brother-in-law lived here?"

"Yes." Her nails had been redone. Yesterday they'd been painted in broad vertical stripes; today they were dotted with silver sprinkles. She curled her fingers and slid her thumbnails back and forth over her pinky nails. "That goes back a long time—over twenty years," Celia said. "Bernie had a room on the second floor. I can't even show it to you—we had the whole place gutted and redone."

"How long have *you* been here?"

"Since we got married—twenty-eight years. Sol's folks were alive then; we moved right in. We had like a little apartment in the attic. When we had our kids we were really on top of each other. We were always planning to move, but then his folks passed away, and Bernie went off to college, so we just stayed."

"When Bernie finished school, he didn't come back here."

"No." Celia scratched behind Pippi's ear, under the silver ribbon. "He lived by himself."

"At the Lantern Light," Nikki said.

She caught a subtle change in Celia's face at the mention of the theater, a glimmer of emotion. Fear? Or was it something else? Celia's fingers worked busily, rubbing her nails with spiderlike secrecy.

Sol said, "Get through with this already, so we can go to sleep."

Nikki said, "I guess Bernie wanted to be at the theater."

Celia's ears turned pink; her cheeks showed smudges of mauve. "The theater was all Bernie cared about," she said. "His first and only love. That and drugs."

"Did you ever go down to one of his shows?" Nikki asked.

"No."

Sol said, "Is this gonna go on all night?"

There had to be *something* else she could ask. She hated to leave—they knew something. There were secrets in the room so real she could almost see their shapes, touch them.

"Does the name Peter Maynard mean anything to you?" she asked Celia.

"Who is he?"

"Director of the Lantern Light."

"Never heard of him."

Dave said, "How about a man named Bienstock?"

"Nix on that one, too," Celia said.

Dave rose, and Nikki followed him to the door. She'd learned nothing. She felt as though what she needed to know lay just outside her reach, tantalizingly close.

"I forgot to mention one thing," she said. "It seems Mr. Zaporelli was more than just a boyhood friend of Bernie's—Mr. Zaporelli acted down at Bernie's theater. Under a stage name, Tony Zim. Does *that* mean anything to you?"

Sol jumped in, too quickly, perhaps. "Never heard it before."

Celia's eyes widened for a split-second. "Me neither," she said. But her face had reddened, shaded to the rich color of her hair.

# 23

"They're lying—they have to connect somewhere," Nikki said as they walked to the Chevy. The case was as frustrating as a tangle of yarn; strands kept leading back into the center of the knot. She had a sudden frightening thought. What if there *wasn't* a real connection between Chaikin's murder and Zaporelli's, only a series of odd coincidences? Eagle-Eye would have her hide; he'd warned her not to dig into the Chase murder, that she'd be wasting her time.

"Tell you one thing," Dave said, "six years ago the Chaikins were barely middle-class and struggling to stay there."

"Did *she* work?"

"Not that I remember. He had the only salary." He opened the door for her, then slipped behind the wheel. "Between then and now they made a lot of money. The house, the clothes—prosperity hit them in a big way."

"I'm starting a credit check on them."

"Let me know what comes up." He turned the key in the ignition and moved out onto Plumb 2nd. They passed two-family brick houses with shades drawn, here and there the bluish glare of a TV lighting a window.

"What happened with your Jane Doe?" she asked.

"Turns out to be the wife of a computer company exec up in Back Bay—maid, chauffeur, the works. A month ago they had a fight and she walked out, wouldn't say where she was going."

"Any kids?"

"Little boy. The husband's heartbroken."

They drove along Gerritsen in silence. She sensed that his meeting with the Boston man had been hard. She'd experienced similar painful moments in her work, knew how it felt to be helpless in a bad situation, unable to make it any better. There was nothing she could say. If they hadn't been at such a rocky point in their own relationship she would have reached over to touch his hand, let him know she understood.

He pulled over at Avenue U. "Drop you at the station?" he asked.

His question jarred her—wasn't he going to take her home so they could talk about the case? She recalled then that he'd said he couldn't handle situations where he was one-on-one with her. Business only, for the time being. Her need to have him there was so great it generated a spurt of anger. "Why won't you stay with me?" she burst out. "Even for a little while."

For a moment he looked at her with sympathy, some of the old tenderness. "I can't put myself through that. I have to know one way or the other where you stand."

Smoke rose from a grate in the sidewalk, drifting up toward the street lamp. "And if I don't *know* where I stand?"

He shrugged but said nothing.

"What if I say no?" she asked.

"Is that your answer?"

"I don't *have* an answer. All I can think about is this damned case—and what's going on between you and me isn't helping."

He released the emergency brake. "I'll take you to the station house."

It wasn't till the next morning, brushing Lara's hair, that she realized he hadn't answered her question.

"Mom," Lara asked suddenly, "are you and Uncle Dave in crisis?"

Nikki laughed. "Where'd you get that idea? Anyhow, what do you mean, crisis?"

Lara studied her with the dark, intelligent glance that reminded Nikki so much of her sister, Iris. "Is it a serious fight?"

"It's not really a fight."

She knew even as she was saying the words that Lara wasn't convinced. The girl was sensitive to every change between her and Dave. She was used to seeing them together more—he'd taken to eating most of his meals with them, coming by early in the morning to make breakfast. If she and Dave went their separate ways, Lara's relationship with him would change too. Young as she was, Lara sensed that. Her niece knew all about losses. She had had practice living through them. Sometimes Nikki felt she would go to any lengths to protect Lara from fresh pain or disappointment. Still, she wasn't ready to let that influence her decision about Dave. What was good for Lara might not be good for *her*.

She slipped a ribbon under the girl's hair and pulled it into a bow. "I'm sure it'll work out." Whistling in the dark, she thought. She didn't feel sure of *anything*.

Her doubts returned as she pulled on her coat. What would Dave be like if they broke up? The all-business, crisp, correct detective he'd been for the past day? Would she start hearing gossip about his love life, rumors that he was seeing other women? The idea chilled her, though she was sure he wouldn't be alone long if they split; he was an attractive man. She left the house feeling gloomy, as though she were looking down a long tunnel with no light at its end.

Glenn Taylor, wearing his black leather jacket and looking hollow-cheeked, ran down the violet steps as Nikki double-parked. She slid over on the seat and rolled down the window.

"Mr. Taylor!"

He sighted her and became very still. "Where's Matt?" he asked.

"Haven't found him yet."

For a split second she could see his control was on the surface, that he was capable of deep rage.

She said, "I have some questions for you."

"How long will they take?" He looked anxiously down the
street, as though part of him had left already. A woman came
out of the building behind him, carrying an artist's portfolio
and a bag of mailing tubes. She wound a scarf around her
neck, the wind lifting an end, pulling at it.

"Mr. Taylor, did Matt show you this picture?" Nikki took
the dual portrait of Chase and Zim from an envelope and
passed it over the window to him.

He blanched. "What about it?"

"He told you it was his father?"

"Yes." Behind the black-rimmed glasses his glance darted
away. "Look, I can't stand here and talk to you. I want to—"

"Did you tell Matt about the trouble at the Lantern Light—
the two deaths?"

"No—I—" He passed the photo back to her, his hand un-
steady. "I don't have time for this. Matt's missing—doesn't
that mean shit to you?"

"Maybe you'd find time at the precinct."

He glared at her. "What do you want to know—how Matt
found out his father was slime? Okay, *I* told him. He showed
me that picture he'd taken from the Lantern Light. I gave him
an article on the place, laid it all out for him. The article said
the cops spent six years looking for Tony Zim. His father, Mr.
Upright Politician, had been involved in a girl's death and never opened his mouth. Walked away from the whole icky mess
like he always walked away from things. You happy now?" A
man pulling into a parking space three cars down looked back
at Glenn as he raised his voice. "If not for me, Matt wouldn't
have known shit. I'm to blame for whatever he—" He broke
off, breathing hard, unwilling to meet her glance.

"What did Matt say when he read the article?"

"Nothing. He didn't say a word. You want to waste your

time taking me in, go ahead. My answer'll still be the same. Okay, lady?"

She watched him run down the street.

All she had so far were bits and pieces, with no idea how they fit together. If they didn't form a picture soon, she could stop worrying about it. Eagle-Eye would take her off the case.

# 24

"I don't know if she's up to seeing you," Elaine Lessing said at the door of the Zaporellis' apartment. "She's having a rotten day." She twisted her watch with a veiny, age-spotted hand.

She looked worn, as though *she* were having a bad day, too. Nikki remembered Donna's temper, her habit of talking to Elaine as though she had no feelings. "Come in anyhow," Elaine said. "I'll go see."

Nikki waited on the gold medallion carpet, admired the grain of the cherry-wood desk. The desk was probably worth more than all Nikki's furniture put together. The room smelled of some pleasant, musky odor she couldn't identify—potpourri, maybe. Her own house had an unidentifiable odor too, but it wasn't potpourri. She'd been straight with Dave—she hated housekeeping, would have spent all her days in a hotel if she'd been able to afford it. He knew that, he'd told her. Anyhow, why was she thinking of him again?

Elaine came scurrying back. "I guess it's okay," she said. She raced ahead, up the oak staircase and past Zaporelli's bedroom, down the long corridor. "She was up all night," she said over her shoulder. "If they don't find Matty soon, she'll end up in the hospital."

Donna's face showed the effects of sleeplessness, dark patches under her eyes. She said to Nikki, "Did you come here to—" She broke off, bit her bottom lip. "Did anything happen?"

"We haven't found Matt yet if that's what you're asking."

Donna lifted her hand, the movement making her wince. "I can feel in my heart that—I just know—" Her eyes filled. Elaine handed her a tissue, and she wiped her tears, blew her nose, every movement painfully slow. "But why isn't he contacting anyone? I saw the appeal on TV. Okay, he doesn't want to talk to me—I can understand that. Why doesn't he get in touch with Glenn? He has no money, you know. He must be sleeping on the street somewhere." She looked at Nikki, terror behind her eyes. "Why isn't he calling?"

In her dark glance Nikki saw what Donna believed—that her son was dead, that that was why no one had heard from him. Nikki said, not fully convinced herself, "These things take time. You shouldn't give up hope." She heard the emptiness of her words. If it were Lara who was missing, she would be inconsolable, wild with anxiety.

Elaine rose, collected Donna's breakfast dishes on a tray, placed the tray on a table, sat next to it.

"Mrs. Zaporelli," Nikki said, "I'm sorry to have to ask you more questions right now, but there've been some developments in your husband's case."

The imperious quality Nikki remembered was gone. Donna said meekly, "What do you want to know?"

"Did you ever hear of a man named Bernard Chase?"

"No."

"His name was Chaikin to begin with. Ring a bell?" She watched for a reaction, but there was none.

"Should it?"

"He was your husband's best friend for years—they went to college together."

"I didn't know any of Dean's college friends."

"Right after graduation the two of them started a theater together, the Lantern Light."

"That's the name Matty was asking about. It's funny—we

got married around then, three, four months after Dean graduated. I never heard him mention the place. Where was it?"

"Off-off Broadway. On Sixteenth Street."

"You're sure it was Dean?"

"Yes."

Elaine tried to stack a cup and saucer on the other dishes
but the cup slipped, spilling coffee.

Donna's glance turned inward, the dark brows knitting together above her fine nose. "He could've gone down there at
night and not told me. He was out all the time; he came in very
late. At first I used to wait up. Then I learned to forget about
him and go to sleep." Her fingers pleated the coverlet. "I
made believe he was next to me. How long was he involved?"

"Six years. He acted in the plays they produced."

Her eyes acknowledged the information. "He always wanted to be an actor."

Nikki said, "It turns out his partner, this Bernie Chase, was
killed too, about six years ago. With the same gun that killed
your husband."

Donna tried to sit up straighter, failed, and slid back on her
elbow. Elaine rushed over to help, but she motioned her away.
"What're you telling me—that you found the gun that killed
him?"

"No, but there's a connection. The bullets in your husband
and the ones that killed Chase were fired from the same gun,
probably by the same person." She kept her eyes on Donna,
saw her fingers shake with a tiny tremor. Donna dropped her
hand and hid it at her side.

Elaine sat down again, hitting the tray with her elbow, rat-
tling the dishes.

Nikki's beeper went off. The number on her screen looked
unfamiliar. "Where can I make a call?" she asked Elaine.

"In my office."

She led Nikki next door to the small sterile space Nikki had seen on her first visit. It looked unused. The computer terminal had been covered and Zaporelli's awards and diploma taken down. She dialed the number.

It was Dr. Akalaides. "Nikki Trakos! What a pleasure! How are your parents? I don't see them no more."

"They retired and moved to Florida. Are you still practicing?"

"Why not? You know what they say, once in the saddle you might as well ride. So you became a police! Perfect for you—a strong body and a good mind. What can I do for you?"

"It's in connection with my work—I'm looking for a place called Sunnycrest, but I'm not sure what it is. It might be a city, it might be a sanatorium. The one thing I know is it's in a dry climate. A doctor recommended it to a patient who has rheumatoid arthritis."

"Sunnycrest."

"That's right." She spelled it for him.

"Okay, I have books I can look in, also people I can call."

"If you get the address and phone number, that would be great."

"I'll try. Nikki, you married?"

She hesitated. He was from the old school, her parents' generation. An unmarried woman was an empty vessel waiting to be filled. Half a person, in search of a mate who would complete her. "No," she said finally, "not yet."

"Good! I was insulted your father didn't invite me to the wedding. Send my regards, your mother, too."

When Nikki came back to the bedroom Donna looked pastier than before, bloodless. She said to Nikki, "Was that—If anything happened to Matt, I want to know—don't protect me."

"That wasn't about Matt. It was about a place your doctor mentioned to me. I'm trying to check on it."

"Fishberg?"

"A place called Sunnycrest."

The muscles around Donna's temples tightened. "I didn't

know you were in touch with Fishberg." The change in her eyes was hardly noticeable, but it was there. A narrowing of her glance, the lids drooping ever so slightly. "It's a sanatorium out west," she said. "I forget exactly where. I asked Fishberg if it would help me to get out of New York and he came up with this place. But I changed my mind—I'd be thousands of miles from Matt—I'd *never* see him. I told Fishberg forget about it."

"Do you have a number for Sunnycrest?"

Elaine put in, "I think—"

But Donna cut her off, said "No," vehemently.

No trespassing, again.

"I guess that's it, then," Nikki said. "Let me try a few names on you before I go. Ever hear of Peter Maynard? He runs the Lantern Light. He took over from Bernie Chase."

"No."

"He never called here?"

"Not that I know of. Elaine?"

"*I* never spoke with him."

"How about a private detective in Brooklyn named Reuben Bienstock?"

"No," Donna said. Elaine shook her head.

Nikki thanked Donna and said good-bye. She followed Elaine through the long hallway, down the oak staircase, back to the gold medallion carpet and cherry-wood desk. "She keeps you hopping," Nikki said.

"That's all right. There isn't enough to do since he died. I like to be busy. I'd look for something else, but she needs me. I couldn't leave her now."

The mention of another job reminded Nikki of a question she'd wanted to ask. "Ms. Royce was talking to me about how you got this job. She said you pleaded with Mr. Zaporelli to hire you, begged him."

"What else did she say? That I promised to stay here for nothing, if only he'd let me? Why does she dream these things up?" She tapped her temple. "She's not all there. I've often wondered why he bothered with *her*. It seems to me she must have had some secret power over him." She stopped for dramatic effect, her lips curving smugly.

"What do you mean?"

"I overheard part of their conversation Tuesday." She blinked several times. "I wasn't eavesdropping, you understand. It was right before I left—I wanted to call the car service. I picked up the phone and they were arguing. He was cursing her—I'd never *heard* him use such language before, and I've heard him angry."

"What was it about?"

She blinked again. "I don't know. Anyhow, she said he was acting like a maniac. That if he thought she was going to go to Brooklyn with him now, he should have his head examined. He laughed and said what made her think he wanted her company. And she told him not to forget what she knew."

"Meaning?"

"I'm not sure. But she said, 'I'm prepared to tell it in the right places, Dean—don't make me angry enough.' And he said, 'Go ahead and tell it—I don't give a—' He said he didn't care."

"Thanks a lot," Nikki said. "I'll look into it."

On her way out Nikki couldn't help thinking that for someone who'd simply picked up the phone to call a car service, Elaine had overheard quite a lengthy conversation.

# 25

Eleven fifteen. She was only three blocks from Karen Royce's apartment. She could go there now, confront Karen with what she'd just learned, ask what it was she'd been holding over Zaporelli's head. But the Mercedes was being searched at two, in the garage of the station house. She had to be in Brooklyn for that. And Eagle-Eye was holding his daily conference on the case at noon. She didn't dare miss this one. If the case had been going better she could have risked it. But Eagle-Eye would be edgy now, Dritzer breathing down his neck, asking why Nikki wasn't producing results. She could just make it if traffic moved.

She headed south on the FDR Drive, merging into the flow of cars, passed the United Nations building, the NYU Medical Center complex. Sunshine caught the sail of a boat on the East River. As the days warmed there would be more boats, families picnicking on the strip along the water, grilling hot dogs on the ribbon of grass.

She guided the car with one hand, thinking back over what Donna had said about Sunnycrest. Donna had asked Fishberg if she would feel better outside of New York, and he'd suggested Sunnycrest; when she'd realized it would take her miles from Matt she'd lost interest in going. But hadn't she realized to begin with that leaving New York would separate her from her son? It didn't make sense that she'd asked about it in the first place. And why had she looked so odd when Nikki had mentioned the name?

Elaine had had the number, Nikki was sure. Why had Donna stopped her from giving it to Nikki?

The Brooklyn Bridge rose ahead, its cables shining like the strings of an instrument. She circled onto the bridge ramp. Fishberg's attitude had been odd, too. Why had he gone on the attack when she'd questioned him about the sanatorium? What was the big mystery?

Halfway across the bridge she glanced to her right at the Brooklyn-Queens Expressway. Her hand tightened on the wheel. It wasn't moving at all. Not even crawling. She'd have to go through the streets, add another fifteen minutes to the trip. With any luck she'd be at the station house at a quarter past twelve, late for the conference. Oh well, late was better than not showing up.

But downtown Brooklyn was a tangle, a honking, snarled sea of cars. She thought of throwing her FBI light on top of the plainclothes Fury, activating the blinkers, but even if she did, there was nowhere to go. The driver behind her had stuck his fist on his horn, causing a deafening bleat. The light ahead was green, but no one moved. It turned red. Still no one moved, but at least the bleating stopped. The second the light turned green the horn started again, the blast echoing through her bones. The guy was a rocket scientist—where was she supposed to go? For an instant she considered getting out of her car, finding out his name and address, making sure he got a noise violation. She gave up the idea as traffic eased a bit.

She crawled along Flatbush Avenue and finally reached a Brownie directing traffic. She rolled down the window, flashed her badge. "What the hell's going on?"

"A demonstration at the courthouse—the six kids that stabbed the principal."

She fought to control her temper.

Twenty minutes later, finally disentangled from downtown

traffic, she tore down Coney Island Avenue with the siren squealing. Maybe the conference had started late. Dritzer himself could have been delayed. Even if she just showed her face. . . .

But Dritzer's car was pulling away as she parked. Eagle-Eye stood at the top of the squad-room steps, waiting for her.

The expression on his face was friendly, almost genial. Her stomach lurched. She would have been more at ease with the familiar constipated squint.

He watched her catch her breath. "No need to hurry, Trakos. Pressure's off now."

Jameson, the only other detective in the room, tried to appear unaware of them, continuing to poke at his typewriter. But Nikki knew he was listening, as was anyone else within earshot.

"What do you mean?" she asked.

"You're off the case."

"What! I'm just—"

"Listen, Trakos—I got a squadful of men working in the dark because you want to play Lone Ranger. You tell me you're going on a wild-goose chase to see a guy named Bienstock. How does he tie in? You got no time to explain. I hold a conference every day and where's my primary? Sorry, she doesn't have time to give us the pleasure. Well, you got all the time in the world now. You're back on the fucking chart."

She'd be back in rotation, catching cases as they came in. How could she persuade him to change his mind?

He strode to his office and shut the door.

"Sorry," Jameson said. He belched lightly.

"Yeah." Was this the thanks she got after two days of grueling work? Eagle-Eye's timing was bad—she'd just begun to feel as though she were getting somewhere.

He was right about one thing—she preferred to work alone. Alone, or bouncing ideas off Dave. And she didn't always communicate. Another black mark against her. It was just that while she absorbed the facts of the case it was distracting to keep reporting back to the squad.

Jameson unwrapped a pack of Rolaids. "Catching again, mon?"

"You heard him." The more she thought about it, the angrier she got. Weren't they impressed that she'd found the link to Chase? They might eventually clear *two* open cases.

Jameson popped a Rolaid into his mouth.

She picked up a blank DD5 form. She should type the results of this morning's interview with Donna, so that whoever took over from her would have the record. The full realization that she was being wrenched off the case and replaced suddenly dawned on her. She stood up and threw the form onto her desk. If she stayed here she might cry, and she'd never done that on the job, not yet. "I'll be downstairs in the garage," she told Jameson. He gave her a puzzled stare. "They're taking apart Zaporelli's car."

"I thought he knocked you off the case."

"I'm not primary anymore," she said. "I can still watch them take apart the car."

She leaned against a pole in the garage as Kinner, the crime scene tech who was an expert on cars, worked on the Mercedes. He dusted the car for prints and chatted about his new boat, a twenty-three-foot Sea Ox with a walkaround, live bait wells, and built-in fish boxes.

She hardly heard a word.

He worked on the glove compartment and the exterior, dug his hand around the upholstery. The whole thing took an hour. Ordinarily she would have begrudged the time, but Eagle-Eye was right—there was nothing to hurry for now.

The Mercedes had no secrets to reveal, no shells. An earring for a pierced ear in the shape of a half-moon lay in a crack of the front-seat upholstery. Kinner bagged it and handed her the bag. Eagle-Eye had forgotten to tell him the case was no longer hers. She felt a fresh sense of loss.

She stared at the earring and thought she remembered a similar earring in one of the pictures of Matt Zaporelli in Glenn Taylor's apartment. No surprise here—Matt's earring could have slipped into a crack of his father's car on any of a hundred trips. It had probably been there for years. Unless it had fallen there on Tuesday, when Matt had gone to Brooklyn with his father and had become angry enough to kill him. But MacFadden, the garage attendant, had seen Matt at the garage of his father's building at seven and again at eight thirty. Could MacFadden have been mistaken?

It occurred to her she should tell her replacement she'd recognized Matt's earring. She ought to go upstairs, do the report, see what else was coming in, find out what her next assignment would be. But she couldn't seem to put any energy behind the idea, couldn't move herself away from the pole.

Kinner finished and turned to another job. Nikki moved sluggishly toward the staircase. No way she could postpone the inevitable—she had to go up, type the report, and put herself back in rotation.

She pushed open the door leading to the staircase, narrowly avoided a collision with Eagle-Eye, who was running down. "Trakos?" he bellowed. His eyes were pinched into their usual glare. "You got lucky."

"How?"

"I'm putting you back on."

She caught her breath, afraid to believe it.

"I'm warning you, Trakos, the least little bit of shit and you're off again. And this time it's permanent. Got me?"

She felt grateful, had an urge to kiss his ugly face. "Got you. What made you change your mind?"

"Your buddy in Homicide called."

"Lawton?"

"Yeah. About a murder in East New York that might tie in to Zaporelli. A friend of yours, Reuben Bienstock."

# 26

The fat man lay in the worst mess Nikki had ever seen, wall-to-wall papers dotted with specks of cat food, streaked with water and blood. File drawers had been opened and searched, their contents dumped every which way on the floor. The ammonia odor was worse than it had been the first time she'd been here. Serrafina, the detective from the local precinct who'd caught the case, had lit a cigarillo. Cops did this to kill really bad stenches they had to work in. In this case the smoke seemed to thicken the closeness, making Nikki want to retch.

From inside a closet, Saddam, the mustached cat, kept up a steady keening sound. He'd been put there to keep him from destroying evidence.

Dave surveyed the disorder. "Perp was looking for something."

Nikki pointed to the scratched red cabinet in the corner from which Bienstock had produced the photographs of Chase, Zim, and Lisa Hirsch. "That one's still closed," she said.

"It's locked."

Meekins, the blond crime-scene tech, said to Serrafina, "Hey, how'm I suppose to take pictures with all this crap around? You can't even see the body."

"Get creative." He puffed on his cigarillo. The cat let out a pained, mournful sound. "D'you have to keep that animal locked up?"

Bienstock had been shot between the eyes; it was hard to

tell exactly how far away the perp had been. Instinctively, Nikki looked for a second wound, didn't see one. Zaporelli had
been given an extra shot after the fatal wound, Chase too. The
single shot to Bienstock's head didn't fit the pattern.

It had happened only hours ago. The landlord, on the floor
above, had heard a shot while he was in the shower. By the
time he'd dressed and gone downstairs—ten minutes later—
the perp had disappeared. He'd called the police, but Bienstock was dead when they got there.

The landlord hadn't seen anyone go into or leave Bienstock's apartment, but he didn't usually watch.

Nikki murmured to Dave, "I know someone who does
watch." While the techs took pictures, she motioned him outside. The boy with the dragon appliqué on his jacket stood
among the crowd outside the ribbon.

Nikki signaled him and he followed them to the corner.

"Yo, what's the rap? It don't look good I'm talkin' to the
Man in front of my buddies."

"Who went in and out of there this morning?" she asked.

He shook his head. "Had a piece of business to tend to, did-
n't get here till just now."

"Big guy with a beard ever visit him?"

"White guy?"

"Yes."

"Kinda sloppy? Built like a football player?"

"That's him." She turned to Dave. "Peter Maynard."

The boy said, "He came a coupla nights ago."

"Monday? Tuesday?"

He thought for a moment. "Tuesday."

That put Maynard in Brooklyn the night Zaporelli was
killed. East New York was less than half an hour from where
Zaporelli's body had been found. "What time was he here?"

" 'Bout half past seven. Come by subway—the people's ex-
press. Stayed 'bout a hour."

That fit in with Dr. Chi's estimate on the time of death.

"He been here before. 'Bout a week ago. Only stay a coupla minutes that time."

Nikki thanked him.

Dave said, "Want me to rough you up a little so it looks good in front of your friends?"

The boy gave him a slant-eyed leer. "No thanks."

The smell inside the apartment seemed worse after the fresh air. Serrafina lit a fresh cigarillo and drew on it deeply. The cat was still wailing. Serrafina complained to the techs, "That's a godawful sound—can't you let the thing out?"

Meekins said, "We shouldna put the fucking cat in the closet. Shoulda stuck him in the oven, turned the gas on."

The dark-haired tech said, "That's what we need in this shithouse, a cat jumping all over everything."

It would take hours to process the scene. Nikki explained to Serrafina she was interested in the red file cabinet, that it contained evidence that connected to her case. "Think I could look at it now?"

"Yeah, the only problem—it's locked."

Dave said, "Let me play with it."

He pulled a key ring from his pocket. Nikki had seen the ring before; it held not only keys but odd-shaped instruments, thin blades with unusual notches. He slipped one of these into the lock. He turned the blade, pulled up on it, and withdrew it partway. There was a sudden click, and the drawer rolled forward half an inch. He opened it fully, then stepped back to make room for Nikki.

The folders were carefully labeled—a surprise for a man who'd seemed so disorganized. She found the one she wanted toward the back of the drawer—"Rose Hirsch"—pulled it out and opened it on the cabinet top.

There were copies of the picture of Lisa, duplicates of the signed double photo of Chase and Zim. Underneath was a clipping from the *Times*, "Mother Seeks Justice at City Hall," a two-column article with a picture. The caption read, "Rose Hirsch, mother of deceased actress Lisa Hirsch, as she waited for the mayor yesterday." The photographer had caught her in profile on the steps of City Hall. She wore a belted coat that emphasized her chunkiness, and though it was raining, she had no umbrella. Her hair had a bright phoniness to it, as though the blond came out of a bottle. She carried a sign that read, JUSTICE FOR LISA. She was a short woman, but there was strength in the set of her shoulders, determination. Something about the picture teased Nikki's brain. Why did so many pieces of this case seem familiar, as though she'd seen them before?

She lifted the article and found a picture of Zim on a rock in Central Park, the Essex House towers in the background. Zim faced the camera, his features clear in bright daylight.

"What do you think?"

"That's our boy Zaporelli," Dave said. "I don't care what he called himself—Zim, whatever. That's him."

Zaporelli was smiling lovingly in the direction of the camera. "I wonder who took the picture," Nikki said.

The cat's wailing had become incessant, frantic.

"What the hell," Serrafina said. He strode to the closet, opened it carefully, and removed the cat. "I'll be right back."

"Where ya going with that?" Meekins asked.

"I'll put him in the car for now, take him home later."

"You're tampering with evidence."

Nikki found only one other item in the folder, a bill made out to Rose Hirsch for "Investigation and Report," in the amount of four hundred dollars. Bienstock had noted that she'd paid the bill, had marked the date.

Nikki closed the folder, then paused, her hand still on it. "Wait a minute," she said, "I think I'm seeing things." She opened the folder again and pulled out the bill.

She hadn't noticed it right away, but it popped out at her now. "Look at the address." She had a strange, haven't-we-been-here-before feeling. "*Weird*," she said. "Twenty-four ninety-three Plumb Second is where Bernie Chase lived. And the Chaikins."

"And I guess Rose Hirsch, too," Dave said.

# 27

Celia Chaikin stared at them, her hand on the open door. "You could have called," she said. Pippi charged back and forth, yelping angrily. The green bows behind the dog's ears exactly matched the color of his mistress's running suit. Jade loops dangled from Celia's ears, swinging each time she moved her head. "Sol isn't home."

"*You* can help us," Nikki said.

She wasn't inviting them in today. Nikki pushed inside, Dave right behind her. Pippi lunged at Nikki's ankles; she felt his tiny teeth, then the beginnings of a run in her panty hose. "Put him away, please."

"Pippi!" Celia said. The dog ran under an armchair, poked his nose out, growled.

Celia stood with them on the pickled oak floor of the entry, rubbed her fingertips over her long lacquered nails in a nervous gesture that made her hands look like claws. Today her nails were a virginal white, almost translucent.

Celia said, "How come—"

"Mrs. Chaikin," Nikki said, "you want to lie to us, it's going to take—"

"I never lied to you." She tried to look indignant, but didn't succeed. The flush Nikki remembered from last night's interview started below her ears and spread to her cheeks.

"You didn't tell us the truth, either."

She wet her lips with the tip of her tongue. "What do you mean?"

Since her first meeting with the Chaikins Nikki had seen Sol as the frightened one, leaning on his wife for direction and support. But Celia seemed shaken now—was it because Sol was out? The commanding general image had faded, leaving an uncertain woman in its place. Nikki opened the folder she'd taken from Bienstock's cabinet, and pulled out Lisa's photo. "Do you recognize her?"

Relief flooded Celia's face. Nikki exchanged a look with Dave. What else had Celia been expecting? Obviously something that frightened her more.

"Lisa Hirsch." Celia reached for the picture, her face softening. "She was beautiful. It's been a real long time." She took the photo, sat in the armchair under which Pippi hid, and motioned them toward other seats. "She lived here with her mother, Rose."

"Why didn't you tell us?"

"Number one, you asked about Bernie, not Lisa."

There was a long pause.

Dave said, "And number two?"

"I feel bad about what happened." She looked up, her eyes misted. "I was the one who gave her Bernie's number, told her to ask him for a job." She looked at the outer door, the skin around her eyes folding into lines of worry. "Sol still doesn't know."

Nikki said, "Doesn't know what?"

"That it was me. It goes back to when Bernie left. His room was empty, so we decided to rent it. Someone—I forget who—recommended Rose Hirsch. She was raising a daughter alone; there were just the two of them, the husband was a no-good, deserted her. She was very neat—I wouldn't have a problem, they said."

"Did you?"

"Are you kidding? Rose was Mrs. Clean. The room had to be just so, the kid had to be just so. She had everything figured out. The kid was going to college, she was going to be a lawyer, maybe the first female President. I felt sorry for Lisa. She was just an average kid. Mostly she wanted to have some fun. Rose held her too tight." She laid the picture on the marble coffee table. "I never had a daughter, only sons." Her voice thinned. "When Rose went to work Lisa used to talk to me, tell me things. She wanted to run away, be an actress. She was certainly pretty enough. So one day—God forgive me—" She broke off, her beefy features twisting, searched in a pocket of her slacks for a tissue. She pressed it to her eyes.

Nikki said, "You told her about Bernie and the theater."

"I felt sorry for her—she was fifteen and Rose was still telling her when to stand up and when to sit down. I thought it would be a way out, and it was. She went to live there. She used to come back every now and then, but she wouldn't tell Rose where she was living. The rest you know—Bernie got her hooked on drugs, and in less than two years she overdosed and was dead."

"What about Tony Zim?"

A sudden flash of fear cut through the sadness. "Who was he?"

Dave said, "*You* tell us."

"The name doesn't mean anything—you asked about him last time, didn't you?" She shifted heavily in the chair. "Wait a minute—I think Lisa mentioned him once. That's right. He was an actor down there, wasn't he?"

"That's good, Mrs. Chaikin," Nikki said, "but not good enough. Tell us the rest of it."

Fear sharpened her glance. "The rest of what? There *is* nothing else. I've been walking around with guilt for thirteen years for what I did. I had to watch Rose go bonkers, and all the time I knew I was the cause of it. She lost the one thing in the world that mattered to her, because I opened my mouth."

"She never found out?" Nikki said.

"No. I couldn't tell her. She stayed with us for a couple of years while she was trying to get the cops to say Lisa's death wasn't just an overdose. After a while she seemed to accept it and give up."

Nikki wondered whether that was true. At some point Rose had hired Bienstock to get more information for her; would she have done that if she'd given up?

Dave asked, "What happened to her?"

"She just took off one day, without a word. I thought she'd be back because she left most of her things—her clothes, her books—but she never showed."

"No note or letter?" Nikki said.

"Nothing. But Rose was odd anyhow—she was never close to anyone but Lisa. I reported her missing. Not because I cared—it was the right thing to do. But they couldn't find her. After a while I got rid of her stuff." She looked at Nikki hopefully. "Are you through?"

"I want to leave you something to think about, Mrs. Chaikin. If there's anything you haven't told us—about Tony Zim, for instance—we'll find out anyhow." She watched hot color creep up the woman's cheeks. "And then we'll be back. It's as simple as that."

"You can't frighten me," Celia said.

In spite of Celia's bravado, Nikki saw she *had* frightened her. Somewhere inside Celia was a well of terror; any mention of Zim seemed to bring up buckets of fear.

# 28

Nikki came back to the station house, careful this time to sit down with Eagle-Eye and explain to him again how Bienstock connected to Zaporelli. He was getting it but not quickly—she could see by his puzzled look. She told him again, trying hard not to lose patience, finally saying, "You'd better push Ballistics to check the slugs in Bienstock."

"You think the same perp did Zaporelli?"

"Could be." There had been no shell casings when she'd left the crime scene; she didn't expect any would be found. The perp had fired at Bienstock's head—the hit was right between the eyes, almost the same spot where Zaporelli had been shot. The killer had known where to aim to be sure to kill, not simply wound. He'd probably had marksmanship training. He'd gone in, done it fast, and gotten out before he was seen. Clever and careful.

*If* it was the same killer. The single shot bothered her, the break from the pattern. Killers, like everyone else, had a distinctive way of operating and seemed to leave a signature on their work.

Eagle-Eye said, "Didn't you just tell me the same gun hit this Chase, the Nose Job? That would mean the perp did Chase and then held onto the gun six, seven years."

"Everything points that way," Nikki said.

Eagle-Eye frowned. "Just make goddamn sure you get here

for the conference tomorrow. *You* explain this shit to Dritzer, not me." He cleared his throat. "Where you headed now?"

"To the Lantern Light, to talk to Maynard, the director. Someone saw him go into Bienstock's place the night Zaporelli was killed."

She explained that Maynard connected to Zaporelli—he'd called him, had been close to Chase, had seen Zaporelli's son, Matt.

She could see the gears of Eagle-Eye's brain grinding slowly, processing the information. "Just make sure you don't disappear this time. Read me?"

"I read you." She'd lost time reporting to him, but it was better than losing the case.

When she came out of Eagle-Eye's office Stavich was at her desk, his stub of a cigarette trailing smoke up his temple. He lit a fresh one, crushed the old butt between his fingers, and threw it toward the wastebasket. It fell short. "You got a call," he said, "a Dr. Alkaline."

"Akalaides."

"Yeah. The place you asked about—"

"Sunnycrest?"

"He gave me an address—Lomdust, Arizona. And a phone number."

"Thanks. How're you doing?"

He yawned. "Gettin' nowhere fast, trailin' this Taylor around. Out to Kennedy—someone musta told Taylor they saw the Zaporelli kid at the airport. Then down to Battery Park City, another loser. Then the last thing this Taylor does is go to some crazy club on the queer side of the Village—Blue Balls, or somethin' like that. I hadda check him through the window. If I'da gone in, they'da made me before I opened my mouth—I'da been the only straight." He pulled out Nikki's bottom drawer and rested his legs on it. "At least it's over. He went back to work."

"When?"

"Tonight. Works at Bellevue, in the emergency. I *figured* he'd get tired of chasing around, but it took longer than I thought. Maybe he ran outta money."

Nikki dialed the number Dr. Akalaides had left for Sunny-crest. Stavich had scribbled the words, "John Remsen, Direc-tor," under the address. She asked for Remsen and was told he was in a meeting. She explained she was a police detective working on Dean Zaporelli's murder and asked for a return call. "I'll give him the message," the receptionist said, in a tone that promised nothing.

Dave waited for her under the Lantern Light banner. Daylight was fading; long gray streaks darkened the sky. She found her-self stirred by the sight of him, his strong features, shadowed face. He wore a European-cut overcoat they'd shopped for to-gether, a rough tweed that made his eyes look black. This morning, at Bienstock's apartment, she'd been too caught up in the murder to think of him as anything but a fellow detec-tive. But tonight her emotions had taken over again. Was it evening coming on, her thoughts turning to comfort and plea-sure, that made her want him back in the old way? She had to make a real effort to fight her feelings, to focus on the inter-view instead.

"He's inside," Dave said, opening the door for her.

She showed her badge to an usher in the lobby and was tak-en to the small office where she'd talked to Maynard on her first visit. There was no room for three; Dave leaned against the open door frame.

Maynard wore a frayed sports jacket over his shirt and a clean pair of jeans, but he still looked unkempt. He was one of those big men who had trouble looking neat, maybe because of his bushy hair. He kept his voice low. "Why did you come now? There's a performance going on."

"Mr. Maynard," Nikki said, "you lied to me the other day. You said you'd never met Reuben Bienstock."

He frowned. "You never asked me that."

"Did you lie about meeting Mr. Zaporelli, too?"

"Matt?"

"No, his father."

His eyes narrowed. "I never met him. What makes you think I did?"

"Something Karen Royce, his campaign manager, said."

"I called. I tried to see him, but it didn't work out."

"When was this?" Dave asked.

"About a week ago, after his son came here." The sound of light laughter drifted in from the direction of the audience. "I told you Zaporelli's son stole the photo from the lobby. Well, what I didn't say was he recognized his father in the picture, the guy called Zim."

Nikki said, "How? That was a lousy picture."

"I don't know, but he did."

She found herself distracted for a moment. The mention of Matt Zaporelli had teased her brain. Why?

"I got to thinking," Maynard said, "maybe Zaporelli knew something about Bernie's death. I even wondered—" He leaned back in the swivel chair. "The girl who overdosed here—"

"Lisa Hirsch?"

"Yes. Her death wasn't altogether an accident, you know."

"How'd you come to that?" Nikki asked.

"Bienstock told me—the detective from Brooklyn."

"Why'd you go out there?"

"He said on the phone he had something hot. There's no law against talking to someone."

Nikki said, "They found him dead this morning."

His voice rose. "Bienstock?"

"He was murdered." She watched Maynard's reaction. He seemed genuinely surprised.

"Jesus! How?"

"Shot, like Zaporelli. When were you there?"

"About a week ago. He said he had information to sell, but I didn't have enough money with me."

"So you went back on Tuesday."

"Yes." He suddenly seemed to realize Dave had been standing all this time. He offered to get him a chair.

"No thanks," Dave said. "What'd Bienstock tell you?"

"How Lisa Hirsch died. She took an overdose, but she could have been saved. He said the night she overdosed, it was right here at the theater. Bernie was stoned—his usual state—so he couldn't have gotten help for her. But Zim was here. Bienstock said Zim didn't make any calls because he didn't want to get involved with hospitals or cops."

Nikki felt her skin prickle, go cold. "So they let her die?"

"They tried to save her. Zim put her in a tub of cold water. He thought maybe that would bring her back, but it didn't. By then Bernie was coming off his high. When they realized she was gone, they got rid of the body, dumped it in an alley on Little West Twelfth."

Nikki was finding it hard to speak. She felt grateful when Dave said, "So why'd you try to see Zaporelli?"

"After Bernie died, I started thinking about his sudden good fortune. The fact that he'd been able to quit his job and work here full time. I didn't understand how he could do that unless he had some kind of patron—you know, a sponsor. I didn't know who was paying him off or for what. But then Zaporelli's son came and said Zim was his father."

Again, the mention of Matt Zaporelli threw her concentration off. Something Stavich had said tonight tickled her brain—what was it?

Maynard said, "I thought maybe Zaporelli was paying Chase to keep quiet about how Lisa Hirsch died."

"Where did that get you?" Nikki asked.

Maynard frowned. "I thought if something *was* going on, the payer might have gotten tired of the payee."

"In plain English," Nikki said, "you thought Chase was

blackmailing Zaporelli and Zaporelli got sick of paying him, so he killed him."

"It *could* have happened that way."

"Is that what you told Zaporelli when you saw him—that he'd killed Bernie Chase?"

"I never saw him!" He'd raised his voice without thinking. He glanced in the direction of the stage and said in an angry whisper, "I told you I never saw Zaporelli. This Royce woman wouldn't even let me talk to him."

"Tell me about your trip to Brooklyn on Tuesday."

"What is there to tell? I went out to see Bienstock. I stayed about an hour and came home."

"You came straight home?"

"Why? Do I need an alibi?" He looked suddenly defiant. "Next time you want to question me, let me know so I can get a lawyer." He stood.

Dave remarked, "Your Bernie Chase let a lot of shit happen."

Maynard's jaw lifted. "I never said he was an angel. He had his shtick. It was the drugs—we could never keep him off them, no matter what. We threw the stuff out; we hid his money. Somehow, he managed to get more." He put his hands in his pockets. The gesture made him look years younger, like an unhappy schoolboy. "If I'd caught his dealer, I'd've killed him."

# 29

It was quiet in the car as Dave started the motor. "It doesn't make sense that Maynard took Zaporelli out," he said to Nikki.

"No. Because if Chase and Zaporelli were done with the same gun, then Maynard killed Chase, too, and he wouldn't have any reason to. I knew that when I kept pushing him on going to see Zaporelli. I just threw it at him to see what he'd say."

He turned on the headlights. "There could've been two perps," he said.

"You mean someone killed Chase and someone else killed Zaporelli?"

"Yeah."

"Could be," she said, "but it doesn't feel right."

He merged into traffic on Ninth Avenue. As he stopped for a light an ambulance tore through traffic behind them with its siren wailing. She thought of Glenn Taylor, Matt's roommate, who'd gone back to work as a medic tonight. Something clicked in her brain and fell into place. She reached out, put her hand on Dave's sleeve. "Wait a minute—pull over."

He double-parked. "What's the matter?"

"The Zaporelli kid—his roommate's been out of his mind with worry, running around for two, three days, right? Well, Stavich told me tonight he went back to work."

"So?"

"So that's nuts. Unless he's sure Matt's okay. No way he'd go back to work unless he knew Matt was safe. He'd still be looking for him."

"Want to go see the roommate?"

"No," Nikki said. "I want to go see Matt."

He looked at her as though she'd gone crazy. "All you have to do is find him."

"Stavich said the last thing the roommate did was go to this gay club in the Village. I bet that's where Matt is."

"Okay, we try every gay club down there."

"Let's start with the one Matt sang at last fall, the Blue Boy on West Street."

In the front window under the words BLUE BOY CAFE, a large blue neon had been shaped into a human figure. Groups of men, most of them young, many handsome, clustered outside on the sidewalk. They seemed to be in uniform; short zip-up jackets—the preferred material was black leather—and blue jeans.

Dave parked and he and Nikki made their way to the door. Nikki took in the crowd's unfriendly glances and was suddenly aware she was the only woman on the street.

The atmosphere was the same inside. The mahogany bar was lined with men drinking, flirting, jostling one another for room. A bead curtain closed off a back room where a piano thumped out a show tune. No one approached to ask how they could be served or to seat them.

They walked through the rows of tables and peered into the back. A transvestite quartet was onstage, four heavily made-up men dressed as chorines in wigs and strapless gowns, singing to the piano accompaniment. The song was "Ask Me How Do I Feel," from *Guys and Dolls*. A coarse-featured singer in a sequined green dress shimmied to the music, wiggling fake breasts. The tallest, a muscular brunette, glanced at Nikki, smiled and waved his gloved hand in greeting. The blond standing next to him seemed frightened, clutching a red feather boa around his throat.

The men at the tiny tables around the stage clapped and sang along. Dave yelled above the noise, "I just thought of something. If he's been here since his father died, how come no one called us? His picture's all over the city."

"I don't know."

They opened the bead curtain again and walked back to the barroom.

The bartender, short and fiftyish with dyed auburn hair and mustache, was serving the crowd single-handedly, mixing drinks and taking cash. Nikki had trouble getting his attention, but when she showed her ID his eyes snapped open. "Wait a minute," he said. He lifted the phone on the mirrored back wall, spoke into it for a moment, then came back.

Nikki took out a photo of Matt Zaporelli. "Seen him around?"

He lifted the photo out of her hand and stepped back into better light. "He looks familiar." He stroked his mustache, handed back the picture. "He's been in, but not lately." Why did she get the feeling that he was lying, that his speech had been rehearsed. "Get you something?" he asked.

Dave said, "Cut the bullshit, mister—who'd you call just now?"

"Call?"

Dave reached across the bar, grabbed the man's shirt. "Where is he?"

Nikki heard the quartet start another song. She had a sudden insight and understood how Matt had been able to stay at the Blue Boy without being recognized. "Let him go, Dave. Matt's singing, that's where he is."

They ran to the beaded curtain again. By the time they got there, only three men stood onstage. The frightened blond singer had gone.

The piano player, thin and pale, was pounding away at "Take Back Your Mink." He stopped playing, looked up at Nikki wide-eyed. The clapping slowed. The room grew silent. "Where is he?" Nikki asked.

The piano player shrugged and rose slowly to his feet. He came up to her chin.

She hooked her foot around his stool, toppled it. That seemed to get his attention. "Where'd he go?"

The piano player's hand shook as he pointed toward a darkened hallway behind the tables. "Down there."

"What's back there?" Dave asked.

"The men's room."

The men's room was empty. Nikki glanced in the stalls and opened the broom closet. She was about to leave when she saw the open window. It had been shoved all the way up, though the night was cold. The wind had blown paper towels off a stack that rested on the radiator, scattering them on the floor. A chair stood in front of the window. On the chair, half hidden under a towel, lay a red feather boa.

She climbed onto the chair and pulled herself through the window. Behind her she heard Dave shout, "I'll get the car."

The window opened on an alley. One end was dark and forbidding, the other hazy with light from the street. She found her pen flashlight in her purse and shone it into the dark. Rats scurried through the garbage, but there was no other sign of life. The end of the alley was sealed.

She sped the other way, toward the street, angry with herself that she hadn't guessed sooner, had given Matt a head start. The alley gave onto West 10th Street. She ran toward its opening, looked in either direction. No sign of Matt. Where would he go? Toward the river, to find a spot along its dark banks. She turned in that direction.

West Street faced the docks along the Hudson. In summer the promenade was crowded with men—couples, or singles looking for a pickup. Today the street was deserted. The wind and chill had driven everyone indoors. Matt was nowhere in sight.

Should she turn left or right? By now he could be far away—if he'd hailed a passing cab, he could be on his way to Queens or Brooklyn. But she didn't think he'd do that. Not in his red girly costume, not if he were trying to hide.

She turned right and headed uptown on West Street. The Chevy came toward her. Dave rolled down the window.

"I'm going to walk north," she said.

"I'll head south, circle back. Watch yourself."

She passed an auto-glass place, a gift shop, a diner, all closed for the night. An apartment building stood tall behind a high fence, its gate locked. An empty parking lot took up the rest of the block, stretching to the corner.

She was about to turn away when passing headlights lit a splash of red against the cyclone fence of the parking lot. She inched closer and shone her flash in that direction. A pair of spike-heeled red patent-leather pumps lay at the base of the fence.

She retraced her steps, backed into the doorway of the gift shop and pulled her gun. She stood in deep shadow and waited, eyes on the fence. The street lamp above it was broken. She squinted, unable to see clearly.

Her heart beat faster. He was nearby. The shoes had hampered him. That's why he'd gotten rid of them.

Minutes dribbled by, as though time were reluctant to pass. Dave's Chevy came down the block. He slowed, but she motioned him on, shaking her head to keep him from stopping. The sound of her own breathing echoed in her ears.

A block and a half away something moved along the fence. She peered into the dimness.

A wispy figure started across West Street, toward the docks. A car passed. In its lights she could see Matt, minus shoes and wig, hurrying toward the water.

She sprinted in his direction. He saw her coming and ran faster. He was moving at top speed toward the river at the end of the docks. Yards behind, she paced herself against him, her breath burning in her throat. Her slim skirt bound her legs with every step she took. She yanked it up around her thighs.

Two concrete barriers separated him from the river. He leaped the first, headed for the second.

She sensed his desperation.

She surged forward with all her will and power. She hurdled the barrier, reached him, and held his arm in a tight lock.

Behind them, Dave's Chevy turned and shone its lights in their direction.

# 30

She smuggled Matt into the station house by a side door and found him normal clothes so he didn't have to be questioned in the costume he'd worn at the Blue Boy. She waited while he cleaned the makeup off his face. He was pale and tired, his skin like ivory. The weariness made him look younger, like a worn child. He kept reminding her of Lara. She thought back to the chase along the waterfront. He'd been headed for the river. Had he wanted to die, or had he just been running away from her?

She brought him into the interrogation room. "I need to ask you some questions, Matt. About the day your father died."

"I don't *have* to answer."

"No." It was nine thirty, and she was beginning to fade. For three nights now she hadn't seen Lara—the kid would forget what she looked like. Plus she had the impossible job of getting used to Dave in his new role as Mr. Perfect Colleague. And here was Pretty Boy Zaporelli, taking the Fifth. He'd made the whole department crazy for days and was now resting on his legal rights. She felt like smacking him.

She had to get him to talk but had no energy to invent a strategy. For half an hour she coaxed him as persuasively as she could. A losing proposition.

"There's no point to holding you," she said finally. His eyes flickered with interest. She was conscious of Eagle-Eye and Dave outside the room, looking through the one-way mirror.

found an unresponsive old woman sunk into her grief. "She could use a visit."

He nodded. His breathing made an audible sound in the quiet room. "I never got along with my dad. And now, I guess—" His eyes filled. He looked at a box of tissues on the desk but didn't take one. He rubbed his fingers along the seams of his jeans. "The paper said they wanted to question me. After all the fights I had with him, I was scared."

"You went underground?"

"I stayed at the Blue Boy. Everyone told me I'd be nuts to go to the cops. I didn't even tell Glenn where I was. But yesterday I saw him on TV, asking me—begging me to call." His voice faded so she could hardly hear him. "He looked terrible."

"He's been worried about you."

"I guess that's why I called."

"Matt, when I was chasing you tonight . . . you were headed into the water." If he was suicidal, by law she had to get him medical attention.

"I was running away. I thought I could—" He stopped suddenly, looking bewildered. "Wait a minute." He frowned. "I was just trying to get away."

She wasn't sure she believed him, but she said nothing.

A car door slammed on the side of the station house. It sounded like Dave's Chevy. Would he leave without saying good bye to her? Maybe he had somewhere to go—an appointment with someone. She had a vision of him pulling up on a street, a woman running out of a doorway and into the car. She dropped the pencil she was holding, watching the point break.

"Tell me about the blowup you had with your father," she said. "It was about the Lantern Light, wasn't it? Maynard, the director, said you came to see him."

"Yeah. He had a picture of my dad in the lobby. In a Mexican costume. At home there was a picture of him in the same costume—I recognized the hat and the little jacket."

"How come you went to the theater in the first place?"

"A couple of weeks ago someone sent me a note."

"Who?"

"I don't know." He fished inside the borrowed shirt and pulled out a money belt. Folded inside was a slip of paper. "It isn't signed."

The note had been written with a felt-tipped pen on a plain white sheet. "Do yourself a favor, Matty," it read. "Go down to the Lantern Light Theater. Find out who Tony Zim was."

"How'd you get this?"

"It came with the regular mail."

Nikki said, "Do most people call you Matty?"

"If they know me well."

That didn't narrow the field much. "Any idea who sent it?"

"No."

"So you went, and you found out who Tony Zim was."

"Maynard told me." His lips tightened. "He said Zim had been in some trouble at the theater years ago, that it had been covered up. It didn't mean anything to me. But when I told Glenn, he showed me an article, how the cops had been looking for this Zim for years. I thought I'd try it on my dad, see if I could get him to open his wallet a little. I told him I knew who Tony Zim was, and he went bananas! He wanted to know how I found out. I wouldn't tell him. I said, either you come through with my grandfather's money or I go to the newspapers. I'll give them some background material they can use when you announce next week." His voice cracked. "He laughed at me, told me I didn't have the balls to try it."

"When were you planning to go to the papers?"

"I wasn't really going to go. I just said it to get a rise out of him."

"Did you know what kind of trouble he'd been in?"

"I knew the Lantern Light had a bad history, but I couldn't figure out how he tied in."

"You went to see this detective, Bienstock?"

"Maynard told me Bienstock had some information. But

Bienstock wanted a hundred bucks, and I don't have that kind of money."

"Bienstock's dead, you know."

He seemed mildly surprised. "He was pretty old."

"He was killed."

His shock looked real, his eyes wide, astonished. "I didn't know."

"So your father got mad when you threatened him."

"He lost it. He smacked me, right across the face." His hand went to his cheek, caressing the spot.

"That's when your mother came down."

"My mother? She was there already. They were having their own battle when I walked in."

"About what?"

"A place called Sunnycrest."

"The sanatorium out in Arizona."

"Is that what it is? You know more than I do. They were giving it to each other real good."

"Do you remember what they said?"

"No—wait a minute. She said, 'I'm not a thing that you can put anywhere you want'—something like that. He didn't answer."

"That was it?"

"I think so. I wasn't paying attention." Pain darkened his eyes. "Why'd he have to sock me?" His voice splintered. "He called me a name. He said I'd never be any good, that I was a queer."

# 31

It was eleven thirty before she finished with Matt and let him leave.

Her glance fell on the printout of Zaporelli's bank account. There were pieces of the puzzle somewhere in those records, if only she understood where. She jammed the folded sheets into her purse. Time to go home. Her brain was too tired to function.

She called Glenn Taylor at Bellevue. "This is Detective Trakos," she told him. "Matt's gone up to his mother's. He said he'd call you from there."

"He going to stay there?"

"For tonight. He wants to be available in case she needs him—at least till after the funeral." She twisted in her chair, looked at Eagle-Eye's empty office. He'd gone home a few minutes ago, disappointed that her interview with Matt hadn't produced more, and as always outspoken about it.

"The reason I'm calling you," she said to Glenn, "I'm a little concerned." She told him how she'd chased Matt along West Street, that she'd been uncertain about Matt's intentions as he ran toward the water. "He said he was just trying to get away, but I'm not sure. Seems to me he could use some counseling at this point."

"I *begged* him to see someone. He didn't want to give me any extra expense."

"I understand money won't be a problem now."

"I'll push him on it. Thanks for calling."

She stood up, stretched, and yawned deeply.

Outside, the wind had died down but it was ten degrees colder. She slid into the Camaro, noticing that Dave's Chevy was nowhere in sight. She told herself she didn't care, hadn't really been looking for him.

She woke Mrs. Binsey up and sent her home, checked to make sure Lara was asleep, brewed herself a cup of spearmint tea. She propped the Federated National printout against the napkin holder and read it again while she sipped her tea.

Three thousand a month. Her gut told her it was funny money—blackmail. But that didn't make sense. Logically, Chase was the one Zaporelli would have paid off after Lisa Hirsch's death. But Chase had scrounged for six years afterward, struggling to manage the theater while he held a daytime job. Only in the last year of his life had money been easier—if he'd been blackmailing Zaporelli, why had he waited six years to do it?

Two-thousand-dollar withdrawals until Chase died and then nothing. That made sense. If Chase had been blackmailing Zaporelli, the payments *would* have stopped with Chase's death. But then they'd begun again three months later and had grown to three thousand. Why hadn't the payments ended permanently with Chase's death? Why had they gone up?

She heard a noise behind her. Lara came into the kitchen, rubbing her eyes.

Nikki hugged her. "What're you doing up?"

"I went to the bathroom."

It wasn't unusual for Lara to get up to go to the bathroom during the night. When life was running smoothly, she went right back to sleep. Otherwise she'd come see if Nikki was home. Sometimes she'd tell Nikki right away what the problem was. Today she was silent, resting her head on Nikki's shoulder. She'd grown so tall this past year—she seemed to be all legs. Iris, Lara's mother, had been short and doll-like. Nikki had begun to wonder whether Lara had genes similar to her own, whether she would grow to be as tall.

She ran her palm over the golden curls. "You all right?"
Lara shrugged.

Nikki said, "I don't want to push you, but I'm blind tired and I have to get up early again. Is there anything you want to tell me?"

"I was thinking about Uncle Dave."

"Nothing's new, if that's what you want to know."

"Oh." The weary sound added at least a decade to Lara's age. "If you ... if you break up, does that mean— He promised to help me make a cake for Easter."

"No matter what happens, you'll see him. He's *your* friend, too." But it won't be the same, Nikki thought.

Nikki walked her back to bed and tucked her in.

She lay in her own bed missing him, his touch, his words. This is what I want, she kept reminding herself. To be my own person, live the life I was meant to live. I just have to get used to it. Weariness took over and she drifted off to sleep.

She opened her eyes two and a half hours later, glancing at the clock. Two thirty. She'd beaten the alarm by three hours.

She was wide-awake, her brain churning as though it were a fax machine receiving a message.

She crept out of bed. The bank printout was still on the kitchen table. She glanced back at the first two-thousand-dollar withdrawal, noted the date. It was seven years ago, exactly one month before Zaporelli had announced he was running for city council. Chase had waited till Zaporelli was about to become a public figure, had blackmailed him then. Or perhaps he'd tried before that; Zaporelli might have refused till he felt he had something important to protect—his voter image.

And the jump in payments? Why had the amount gone up another thousand three months after Chase's death? Was it possible to have a new payee in an old blackmail situation? A payee with more ambitious ideas than the original blackmailer?

Nikki didn't have the answers to these questions, but she could guess who might.

# 32

Karen Royce's apartment building was less luxurious than the Zaporellis', though it was only three blocks away. There was one doorman instead of the army of red-jackets, two elevators and not ten.

It was still early. Karen wore pale silk pajamas and a matching robe as she ushered Nikki into her living room. Floral prints covered the furniture, in soft colors to complement Karen's blondness. In contrast with the pastels, a row of dark antique firearms had been mounted on the wall. Nikki walked closer, looking at a long-barreled antique revolver, its frame intricately carved, its grip made of bone.

"I come from a hunting family," Karen said.

"You shoot?"

"Sure, since I was a little kid."

Nikki sat opposite her on the sectional. Karen's skin was flawless even without makeup. Bright morning light shone on her hair. If there had been any dark roots, Nikki would have seen them clearly. Maybe she'd been wrong, and Karen *was* a natural blonde. If so, her hair color was the one honest note about her.

"Last time," Nikki said, "I asked you about the monthly withdrawals Mr. Zaporelli made—"

"I told you—he didn't give that money to *me*."

"Right. What you didn't tell me is that those were blackmail payments."

Karen bent forward to the coffee table and moved a brass frog squatting on its surface.

"Did you know it was blackmail?" Nikki asked.

"I found out a year ago." She straightened up, pushing her hair behind her ears.

"Who was blackmailing him?"

"These people in Brooklyn—I never found out why. We'd drive to Brooklyn every Tuesday to see his mother. I noticed that once a month—the same day I picked up the cash—we'd make an extra stop at this other house. He'd take an envelope with him when he got out of the car, come back without it. I didn't want to ask what it was all about—he didn't like a lot of questions. But I was curious. Through a friend at the phone company I got the name and number of the people who lived there."

"Who was it?"

"A couple named Chaikin."

Nikki had sensed she wasn't through with the Chaikins. She'd expected the case to twist around and come back to them again.

"I called one day," Karen said. "It was right before one of the payments. I got the wife. I said, 'Tell Mr. Chaikin Mr. Zaporelli would come by with the money at the usual time.' She sounded surprised, but she didn't say, 'Who is this—what's it all about?' She knew. When Dean went in they must've told him about the call, because when he came out, he was boiling. Told me not to stick my nose where it didn't belong. I asked him what he was paying them off for. He said insurance. I didn't really understand, but he wouldn't explain."

Karen hadn't understood, but Nikki did. Zaporelli was paying money to insure his future against the ugly secrets of his past. Everything in the puzzle pointed backward—to Tony Zim and the Lantern Light, to the sad, needless death of Lisa Hirsch.

Karen lifted her fingers to push her hair behind her ears, discovered it was there already, and dropped both hands into her lap. "I asked him what would happen if he stopped paying them. He said he couldn't just stop, but he had a plan. He was going to buy a gun—no bullets, just a gun—and threaten them with it, frighten them into backing off."

That explained the .38 in the glove compartment and why no bullets had ever been bought for it.

Nikki said, "You held the blackmail over his head on Tuesday, didn't you?—said you'd tell what you knew about him."

"How did you—" Karen broke off suddenly, her lips pressing together. "Elaine must've listened in. Dean and I were fighting about the timing for the divorce—the usual. I was impatient. I pushed him too hard and he got nasty."

"What did he say?"

"I don't remember." But Nikki could see from the quick shift of her glance that she *did* remember. "So I threatened to tell what I knew about the Chaikins. He hung up on me."

"Is that the last time you talked to him?"

"No. I called back about five minutes later and told him I wasn't going to Brooklyn with him." She smirked. "I'm sure Elaine listened in on that one, too."

"And then?"

She hesitated. "I went home and got rip-roaring drunk."

According to the doorman and the garage attendant there was a six-hour gap in her story. Nikki didn't want to bring that up now. She had a more urgent question.

"The name Sunnycrest, Miss Royce. Does it mean anything to you?"

Even before she answered, Nikki could see the change in her complexion, the rosy tint rising to her forehead, the bright spots in her cheeks. "It's a sanatorium out west. Dean was looking into it for his wife."

"*Mr.* Zaporelli was looking into it? His wife said *she*'d become interested in it."

Her forehead knotted, then relaxed as she smiled. "Maybe that's what she has to say."

"What do you mean?"

"Nothing, really." She lowered her glance to the table again and moved the frog back to its original position. "It was just a place Dean had some correspondence with. Maybe he called once or twice. Nothing special about it."

Then why, Nikki wondered as she rode down in the elevator, had Karen blushed so hard? Why hadn't she been able to meet Nikki's eyes when she'd talked about the place?

# 33

Nikki unsnapped her holster as Dave pressed the button on the electronic monitor. You never knew when you'd need your gun; it was smart to have it handy. Sol Chaikin's voice squawked through the box, "Who is it?" Down the block a man walked around his white picket fence and picked up papers blown against it by the wind.

"Detective Trakos and Detective Lawton," Nikki said.

"I don't believe it!" The release buzzer sounded.

By the time Nikki and Dave reached the door Celia had joined her husband. "We don't have to let you in," she said. "There are laws."

"It's harassment!" Sol exploded.

Nikki eyed them coolly. "Want to file a complaint? You tell what *you* know, then it's our turn."

The corners of Sol's eyes creased with worry. "What do you mean?"

"We'll tell them how you paid for all this." Nikki gestured toward the interior, the pickled oak floor, display cabinets, soft modern lighting. "It's interesting, Mr. Chaikin, you had the house redone—must've cost you a pretty penny. Yet you paid for it all up front. No mortgage on your credit check, no home-improvement loan." She took a chance, said, "I called the contractor who did the work. He loved you—cash on the line."

Sol seemed to wilt, but Celia said, "I don't know what you're talking about." Her fingertips rubbed against her nails in their private ritual dance.

Dave said, "Mind if we come in?" Without waiting for an

answer he walked past them into the living room. Nikki followed.

Sol drew himself up, tried to look taller. "You'd better explain."

Dave said, "It has to do with your brother Bernie. Here's how I see it. Bernie dies. After a couple of months you go through his stuff. You're a math teacher—you put two and two together. Your brother's been getting a gift from a friend, two thousand bucks a month. You decide *you*'re going to get the gift now, like an inheritance Bernie passed on. Except it's not going to be *two* thousand. You put a little pressure on the donor, and lo and behold—it's *three* thousand."

"You can't prove—"

"Sol, let me handle this," Celia said. "Go on with your story, officer."

"You get this gift for five years. But the donor starts feeling the pressure. Maybe he's got expenses he didn't expect—like a campaign for assemblyman, for example. One day he tells you he's not going to pay anymore. And to back it up, he pulls a gun, threatens you."

Sol moved so that he and Dave were head to head. "What're you saying?"

"That you didn't like his pulling the gun, so you went and got your own—"

"Are you nuts! You know what—"

"Don't answer him!" Celia said.

"He can't stick me with this crap! I didn't kill him. With *what* should I have killed him? I don't own a gun."

Celia directed her words to Nikki as though Nikki would be more reasonable than Dave. "Why should Sol kill him? He was the goose that laid the golden eggs."

"Something else," Sol said, his jaw thrust toward Dave. "You told me last time that Chase and Zaporelli were killed with the same gun—are you saying I killed my brother? My own brother?"

"Maybe you got wind of the blackmail *before* he died," Dave said, "and you thought—"

Sol leaped at him, hands aimed at his throat. Dave raised his knee as Sol came close. He connected with Sol's middle. The wind went out of Sol. He groaned and slumped into a chair. Celia knelt at his side but he pushed her away. "Don't ever say that again," Sol croaked as soon as he could speak. His eyes had filled, whether from emotion or pain Nikki couldn't be sure. "My own flesh and blood—what do you think I am?"

Nikki said to Celia, "Zaporelli came to see you last Tuesday?"

"That part's true. But he never gave us the money. He said he was tired of paying, that he had too many other things coming up, that he was going to stop." Her eyes widened. "He had a gun, like the officer said."

"Last Tuesday's payment—"

"We never got it." Nikki gave her a hard look. "I swear—he never gave it to us. Next morning I was walking Pippi and I saw his car. I couldn't understand why it was still in the neighborhood, in a deserted place like that. So I looked in."

She was calm this time, calm enough to be telling the truth. Earlier, when she'd lied, there'd been hot denial behind her words. "What exactly did you have that was worth paying for?" Nikki asked.

Celia went into the next room and came back with a manila envelope. "Sol found these when Bernie died."

Sol said, "They were separate from his other stuff, just the way you see them."

Nikki pulled out a set of publicity photos showing Zaporelli and another actor onstage. "That was taken the night Lisa died," Sol said. "It proved Zaporelli was at the Lantern Light on that date. Bernie hid the pictures to protect Zaporelli. Later he must've figured out they were worth something."

Under the first set of photos was a group of smaller candid

shots snapped outdoors in Central Park. They looked as though they'd been taken the same day as the photo Nikki had found in Bienstock's file. She recognized the Essex Towers in the background. Zaporelli wasn't alone in these shots. He stood with his arm around Lisa; she gazed at him tenderly.

"She was crazy about him," Celia said.

"The man was an animal," Sol put in. "Lisa was pregnant when she died; it must've been him. And here he was, a married man. How do you do that to a young girl? When she was dying, he didn't lift a hand to help her." He shook his head, lips tight. "He got what he deserved."

He said, "She used to live here, you know. She moved away—at the time, nobody knew where." Nikki glanced at Celia, but she averted her eyes, examining a piece of lint on her sweater. Sol said, "Her mother, Rose, was still here when she was killed. She went bonkers."

"In what way?" Nikki asked.

"She never got over it," Sol said. "She woke up in the morning thinking about Lisa, went to bed at night thinking about her. Like the misery kept the kid alive for her, know what I mean? She wouldn't give it up."

# 34

Everything pointed to the past, like a circle that hadn't been closed.

Nikki could hardly contain her excitement as she ran up the station-house stairs. She almost had it solved. It was falling into place fast now, a complicated structure with only a few missing parts.

Dave had dropped her off and had gone back to Homicide. A copy of the ballistics report for Bienstock lay on her desk. He'd been killed with the same gun as Chase and Zaporelli. But not mutilated. No extra shot after death, like the one to Chase's nose or Zaporelli's genitals. Why not? Why did that seem important?

She called Sunnycrest again and got the flat-voiced receptionist. "Mr. Remsen's in a meeting. I can't interrupt him."

"It's urgent."

She heard a sigh on the other end. "I'll try to get a message to him. Call you back." The line went dead.

Stavich came in, panting after his walk up the steps. The odor of tobacco drifted across the desk. He jerked his head in the direction of Eagle-Eye's office. "Goin' in?"

For a moment she was puzzled, then remembered the daily conference was about to begin. The thought of wasting a half hour with Stavich, Eagle-Eye, Dritzer, and the other brass sickened her. Not now, when she almost had the answer. "Be there in a minute," she said.

She thought of explaining to Stavich how the case was breaking. Would he understand? Suddenly she was missing Dave again. She realized she'd been missing him on and off for days, not only at night in bed, but in the late evenings and during the day. It was getting worse, not better.

"See ya inside," Stavich said.

"Right."

Dritzer came up the stairs, marching past without even a glance in her direction, and went into Eagle-Eye's office.

The phone rang. "Detectives, Trakos speaking."

"This is Mr. Remsen, Sunnycrest Farms." Remsen spoke quickly, sounded impatient. "I understand you called?"

"Yes. You had an inquiry from a Mr. Zaporelli recently?"

A short silence. Remsen said, "I can't discuss that with you."

"Mr. Zaporelli's been murdered, Mr. Remsen. Did you know?"

"No, I didn't. That still doesn't change our policy. We don't give out information about our clientele or even about prospective clients. Our clients come from the upper echelons of society. Our policy has always been to protect—"

"I'm not sure you understand. This is a police matter."

"That makes no difference."

"Okay, Mr. Remsen. I'm puzzled, but when I hang up, I'll call the local sheriff's office, and maybe the sheriff can explain it. Or maybe he can drive over to Sunnycrest so he can make it clearer." A longer silence, only the sound of breathing in her ear. "Mr. Remsen?"

His voice dropped an octave; he sounded annoyed. "What do you want?"

"Who made the inquiry, and when?"

"Miss Karen Royce. All our correspondence was with her, as an agent for Mr. Zaporelli. It must have been two months ago she made the first call."

"Asking for placement for Mr. Zaporelli's wife?"

"That's right, Donna Zaporelli. And a companion, Ms. Lessing."

Eagle-Eye came to the door of his office and eyed her impatiently. She signaled she'd be there soon and he retreated. She said to Remsen, "What happened with the placement?"

"We accepted her, of course. We returned the signed agreement papers to Miss Royce last week."

"What kind of facility is Sunnycrest?"

"Long-term care. Most of our clients live here for years. According to her medical records, Mrs. Zaporelli requires round-the-clock nursing at times. We would be able to supply that kind of care during her bad spells. Mrs. Zaporelli was to start her stay with us next Monday, but she called and canceled two days ago."

"Miss Royce called?"

"No, Mrs. Zaporelli."

"She said she'd changed her mind?"

"She didn't give any reason. Just canceled."

"Thank you, Mr. Remsen. You've been very helpful."

She replaced the receiver as quietly as possible. She could get across the room and down the steps without Eagle-Eye seeing her. He'd be angry, but she couldn't sit through a conference. Not now, when she had the answer almost in her hand.

She'd reached the top of the staircase when she heard him behind her. "Where the fuck're *you* going?"

She wanted to say she was going out to get the murderer, but he wouldn't understand. "Be right back," she called.

"Don't fuckin' bother. Get your ass in here now or I'll—"

The door slammed behind her, cutting off the sound.

# 35

The car flew back to Manhattan as though it knew the way. Nikki's hands and feet guided it, her mind busy. Why had Bienstock been killed? His murder wasn't the same as the others, yet he'd been shot with the same gun. Who would have benefited from his death?

And then she knew. It was almost too bizarre to believe. Yet in the year she'd worked as a detective she'd learned to trust her instincts, to follow her mind where it led.

If she'd figured it out, Matt might too. And if he spoke to the wrong person, said too much— She was suddenly afraid for him.

She stopped at a phone stand on Third Avenue and dialed Zaporelli's apartment. Elaine answered.

"This is Detective Trakos. Is Matt there?"

"He went downtown to meet Glenn for lunch," Elaine said. "He should be back soon. Any message?"

"No, thanks."

He was due back soon. That gave her a little time, but not much. She rushed back to her car.

Karen had changed out of her silk pajamas. She wore a black suit with exaggerated shoulders and an abbreviated skirt. Her eyes widened in surprise when she saw Nikki.

"Not again!"

"The last time."

Nikki stepped into the space that served as both entry and dining room. "Mr. Remsen at Sunnycrest had an interesting story to tell." Karen turned pale. "I want to hear it from you."

Karen reached behind her, pulled a high-backed chair away from the table, and sat down. "I did a lousy thing."

"When?"

"Tuesday. The day Dean got killed." She swallowed, glancing at Nikki from under her eyelashes. She pushed her hair behind her ears. "Dean lied to me. He told me he'd gone to see his attorney about the divorce, that it would be complete soon. I don't know what got into me—I checked on him. I called the lawyer and said Dean was wondering where the divorce papers were. He said, 'What divorce papers?' Dean hadn't even spoken to him about it. I couldn't believe it!" Angry tears sparkled in her eyes. "For two months I'd been working on a placement for Donna at Sunnycrest. Suddenly I saw what Dean's plan was. He wasn't going to divorce Donna—too messy with the election coming up. He would send her to Sunnycrest and get her out of the way. I called Dean and—I really lost it. I told him he'd never intended to get a divorce, never intended to marry me, had only been using me. He said—" Her eyes brimmed over, and she had to stop to get a tissue. "He said to fuck off." She blew her nose. "I wanted to do something to hurt him, the meanest thing I could think of." She looked down at the table. "He'd been keeping the Sunnycrest arrangements secret. He said he wanted to tell Donna in his own time and his own way. I took the signed agreement papers and all the correspondence and I messengered them over to her. When he came home he phoned me. He—" She choked on her tears.

Nikki waited impatiently. "What did he say?"

"That he wanted out of the relationship. He called me names, told me to look for another job. So I did—at any rate I tried to. I called this politician in Queens who was always talking about running against him and said I wanted to see him. I was going to offer my services, give him all the dirt I had on

Dean—and I had plenty. I made an appointment with the guy—you can check on it, I'll give you the number. I drove out there and sat in front of his house for hours. But I just couldn't bring myself to go in."

"Anyone see you?"

"This woman came out of one of the houses after a while, asked if I needed help. I guess I was crying. She would probably remember me. I don't know how long I sat there. I drove back home and made my way through two bottles of Scotch. Next morning, when I turned on the radio, I heard about Dean." Her lip trembled, making her look like a little girl. "If he'd lived, we'd have made up. We were always fighting, patching it up. That's what it was, a lover's quarrel." Her eyes pleaded with Nikki, begged her to say it was so.

# 36

The sun had slipped behind the buildings, turning the light to gray. Nikki wondered whether to take the car, made a snap decision, and raced the three blocks on foot to Zaporelli's building. Had Matt come home? She flashed her badge at the red-jacket behind the desk and walked slowly to the elevator, knowing she would attract more attention if she ran. Alone in the elevator, she slipped her .38 into her waistband where it was easier to get at. She buttoned her jacket over it. It occurred to her, too late to do anything about it, that she shouldn't have come here alone. There might be trouble, even shooting.

Elaine answered the door. When she saw Nikki her forehead creased. "You didn't say you were coming."

"Is Matt home?"

"No." She blocked the way. "I'll tell him you came by."

"Actually, it's his mother I want to see."

"This is the fifth or sixth time! Are you trying to make her sick?"

Nikki didn't answer. She waited till she stepped aside.

Shaking her head, Elaine led her past the living room and up the oak steps. "She gets upset the minute she hears you're coming, when the desk buzzes her."

She ushered Nikki into Donna's room and took her place next to the bed in watchdog position. Donna lay on the bed, fully clothed in slacks and sweater. She smiled weakly at Nikki. "Thanks for finding Matty."

"Glad we could."

Nikki was relieved that Matt was out. His balance was fragile; he didn't have to be present to hear accusations, watch her make the arrest. She said to Donna, "I spoke to Mr. Remsen at Sunnycrest Farms this morning."

Donna's face turned a shade of gray.

Nikki said, "It must've felt good to cancel the placement."

"It was the greatest moment of my life. Wherever he is, I hope Dean heard me do it. He had me by the short hairs. I didn't have a nickel of my own, and he was sending me out to nowhere. I couldn't just say, I won't go."

"You wouldn't have seen Matt—"

"I would *never* see Matty. Dean didn't give a shit. Just wanted me out of the way." She tried to sit up, winced.

Elaine's eyes followed every move, her mouth tight with anxiety. She said, "How much more of this can she take?"

Nikki looked past her and said to Donna, "You told him you'd seen the agreement?"

"Damn right! I said, I'm no piece of furniture you can move out of your way—I'm human." She laughed bitterly. "The whole thing was a secret—can you believe it? Goldilocks knew; she made all the arrangements."

Nikki said, "Mr. Zaporelli wasn't sending you out there alone. He'd made arrangements to send Elaine with you."

She gave a short laugh, said contemptuously, "Elaine!" Her chest rose and fell, her breathing shallow.

Elaine sprang up, glared at Nikki. "You go on this way and she'll have an attack."

Nikki turned her full attention on the older woman. "The Sunnycrest arrangement came as a surprise to *you*, too."

"Of course it did."

"You thought you'd have more time."

Elaine's glance narrowed. She blinked several times.

"Isn't that right?" Nikki said.

The phone rang. Elaine ran into the hall. "I'll get it in the office." Nikki followed, leaning against the door frame. Elaine said into the phone, "That's right. At three. La Guardia. Yes, a station wagon."

When she hung up, Nikki said, "Going somewhere?"

"Back home—Cincinnati."

Nikki lifted an eyebrow. "Mrs. Zaporelli laid you off?"

"No, I quit. I told you, there isn't enough for me to do."

"Or maybe you did what you had to."

Elaine turned so that she faced Nikki fully. "What do you mean?"

"The three people you killed."

She grew perfectly still. "You'd better explain yourself."

"Okay. What do I call you—Elaine? Or Rose?"

A tiny spark flickered behind her glance. "Who's Rose?"

"Rose Hirsch. The mother of a beautiful, talented girl named Lisa. Who was killed—by accident or maybe neglect." Elaine's face was masklike. A muscle tripped up and down in her eyelid. She reached up, trying to rub it into submission.

Nikki said, "The only thing Rose cared about was getting even with the people who let her daughter die. The cops let her down, so after a few years she hired a detective, Reuben Bienstock, to find out who was responsible. He told her Lisa had been involved with two men at the theater she worked in. One had her hooked on cocaine, the other was sleeping with her. These two had been with Lisa the night she'd died, had done nothing to prevent her death. He came up with their names—Bernie Chase and Tony Zim. He dug up Zim's real name, Dean Zaporelli.

"Rose was a heavy blonde, who'd gotten a lot of publicity when her daughter died. She was afraid she'd be recognized, so she lost weight—lots of it—and let her hair grow in to its natural gray. She took a phony name. She even changed the way she spoke, trained herself so no one would guess there was any Brooklyn in her, told people she came from Cincinnati. Then she wormed her way into the first man's life—Chase. She found work at his office, his day job. When he trusted her completely, she killed him. It took years. But that made it even better. She could think about her revenge every day, plan it."

"Fascinating. I know you'll forgive me if I can't really listen. I'm winding things up today."

Yet she made no move to push past Nikki. She stood stiffly with her back against the desk as though held there by some invisible force, hands gripping the edge.

"When she'd finished the first murder, Rose changed identity again and went after the second man." The stillness in the apartment was complete. Was Donna listening? If so, Nikki prayed she would stay in bed, wouldn't complicate things by trying to help. "On Tuesday, when you saw the Sunnycrest agreement, you realized you wouldn't have too many more chances to kill Zaporelli—you'd be in Arizona with Donna. That afternoon you went downstairs as though you were leaving for the day. You knew he'd be alone—you'd overheard his fight with Miss Royce, heard her call back and tell him she wasn't going to Brooklyn with him. You waited outside the garage and asked him for a ride. He made a stop in Brooklyn—you waited patiently. When he came back you directed him to a deserted block—"

"How would I know where to direct him?"

"Because you'd lived there. A long time ago, but the neighborhood hadn't changed that much. You shot him. When he was dead you cleaned up the shell casings, took the three thousand dollars he'd withdrawn from the bank that day, and walked to the Avenue U bus. You knew just where to find that, too. You're a New Yorker, Miss Lessing. Only a New Yorker would know where the old Metropolitan Opera House used to be—that was a bad slip."

From the floor below, Nikki heard a door slam, heard Matt shout, "Hello! Where is everyone?"

Donna screamed over the intercom, "Stay there, Matty! Don't come up—"

Would he listen to his mother? Or come up to see why she sounded so frantic? If he came up, the situation would be infinitely more complicated. If Elaine had her gun with her, she might threaten him. Nikki would have to worry not only about her own safety but Matt's too.

Elaine's eyes shifted, gauging the distance from the desk to the door. She seemed benign, a little gray-haired lady missing only her knitting needles and yarn. But Nikki knew how deadly she was. She watched her every move. Did she have her gun at hand? A careful killer like Elaine would protect herself, keep it nearby.

Elaine's eyes blinked rapidly. "You said I murdered *three* people."

"Chase, Zaporelli—and Bienstock," Nikki said. "I came here yesterday and asked if you knew the name. You were afraid he'd lead me to you; it was too dangerous to let him live. That's what gave me the clue—you were the only one who would have benefited from all three deaths."

She heard Matt's steps on the staircase. Donna cried, "Stay there! Oh God, don't come—"

Elaine's eyes darted to the hallway behind Nikki. Reflexively, Nikki glanced backward. The hall was empty. When she turned back, Elaine's hand was in the desk drawer behind her, groping. Nikki lunged forward, lifted her foot and held it against the drawer. The howl that escaped from Elaine's throat was more animal than human. Nikki opened the drawer carefully to release Elaine's hand, held her wrists in a tight lock, and cuffed her. Inside the drawer lay a black .380 Walther, safety off, ready for action.

# 37

Matt stood in the doorway. "What the hell—"

Nikki said, "Call nine one one. Tell them I need backup right away." He turned and ran toward the bedroom.

She secured the cuffs to the heavy desk chair and pushed Elaine into the chair. She took a seat a few feet away, reached behind, and lay the Walther on a chair. A week ago in Staten Island a cop had been shot with a gun he'd taken from a perp but carelessly left within reach. Last she'd heard, the cop was still in critical condition.

She trained her .38 on Elaine, though Elaine didn't seem to have much fight left. "My hand hurts," she complained.

Nikki said, "Did you know the Chaikins were blackmailing Zaporelli?" Elaine looked ready to say something, then hesitated. "It doesn't matter whether you tell me anything or not." Nikki tilted her head toward the Walther. "When we get your little gun into the police lab, it's going to do all the talking we need." The hard evidence would put Elaine away for the rest of her life, that and a statement Nikki would take at the precinct.

Elaine spent a quiet moment thinking, then said, "I didn't know he even knew the Chaikins. It was funny, pulling up to the house we lived in, Lisa and me. Celia really fixed the place up."

Nikki said, "They'd been taking from Zaporelli for years. Bernie blackmailed him first. When Bernie died, they took over."

DEAD CENTER                    213

"Bernie Chase." Elaine's eyes grew hard. "To begin with, I wasn't going to kill him. I just wanted to see what kind of man he was. I got a job with his company and watched him."

"He didn't recognize you?"

"He'd never met me—I moved into Celia's after he was gone. I was going to go up to him one day and tell him who I was. Tell him what it felt like to lose Lisa. And then I couldn't. You know something—I never could tell anyone what that was like." She stared at Nikki, her eyes glazed as she focused on the past. "I thought about him all the time—how he was free and doing what he loved—just alive. While Lisa—" Her voice crumbled. "I bought a gun and learned to shoot. You'd be surprised what you can learn. At first I couldn't figure out how to get close to him, how I could see him outside the office. I started buying cocaine, selling it to him way under cost."

"How did a straight like you get hold of coke?"

"It wasn't easy, but I did. I became his supplier—top-grade stuff at cut rate prices. When he left the job to work full-time at the theater I kept on supplying him. I'd meet him in out-of-the-way spots—parks, libraries."

"And one day you met him in a motel room at the Modern."

"You got it." Her lips turned up triumphantly. "And when he was dead I marked him, gave him one right where he snorted the stuff."

"Bienstock was the only one you didn't 'mark.'"

"He wasn't the same as the other two—I only killed him because I couldn't take a chance he'd talk. I searched his files afterward, but I couldn't find the stuff on Lisa and me. There wasn't time."

Nikki heard Matt hang up the phone, heard him walk toward the staircase. She said, "Why'd you send that note to Matt?"

"I'd wanted to do something like that for a long time. Make Zaporelli suffer through Matty the way I'd suffered through Lisa. When I saw the article on the theater it gave me an idea. I figured Matty would stick it to Zaporelli, make him sweat."

"He did."

She nodded, satisfaction in her glance. "That's all he talked about on the way out to Brooklyn."

"How'd you get him to take you there?"

"I asked him for a ride, told him I was going to visit a friend. I let him talk the whole way. He liked the sound of his own voice. He was going on about Matty. Matty was ungrateful, was giving him grief. He went to see Celia and Sol. When he came back he started on Matty again. He shouldn't have had Matty, not worth all the misery."

Her mouth twisted to the side. "I had the gun in my lap—I'd taken it out when he left the car. I said, 'My daughter was hell to raise.' He looked over at me. He said, 'I didn't know you had a kid.' 'Her name was Lisa Hirsch,' I said. And then I shot him."

Tears lay on the rims of her eyes. "Did you know," she said, "my baby was pregnant by him when she died?"

# 38

Dave sat up in bed, leaning his elbow into the mattress. "I was home—both nights. All I could think about was how I missed you."

"I missed you, too," Nikki said. "I finally figured out I was asking myself the wrong question. Not do I want to marry you and lose my career, but how can I marry you and still keep my career."

He sucked in his bottom lip, something he did when he was stirred emotionally and couldn't speak. "I'm glad." He traced her features with the tip of a finger. The light behind his bedroom window shade glowed with each passing car. "Your career isn't doing bad," he said.

"The commendation?" She laughed. "Eagle-Eye's telling everyone he was smart to let me run the case my way, that there are certain detectives you have to keep a tight rein on, and others blah, blah, blah. Let's see if my name gets on that promotion list now."

"It's a feather in his cap you caught Lessing. She would've slipped away again, picked up a new identity—she was good at that."

She sat up in bed and leaned against the headboard. "Speaking of slipping away, it gripes me that Celia and Sol Chaikin'll walk away scot-free. They must've hit Zaporelli for over a hundred thousand dollars, close to a hundred and eighty."

"Mrs. Zap doesn't want to press charges?"

"Couldn't care less."

"And the son?"

"Same."

He shrugged. "That's it, then. No complainant, no case." She looked over at the clock. It was getting late. She reached for her clothing. "This is one thing I won't miss," she said. "Getting dressed afterward and going home." He didn't answer. She turned back to look at him. He was sucking in his lip again, the happiness in his eyes unmistakable.

She put down her clothing, smiled. "You'll be sorry. You've never been to a Greek wedding, have you?"

"No."

"They break plates."

"So?"

"And throw money."

"That sounds good."

"And the men put their arms around each other and dance—"

"Wait a *minute*!"

"That's right," she said. "They dance in a circle. It's called a *kalamatianl*. The groom does it too."

"I don't know." His eyebrows peaked, two dark triangles. He pretended to worry. "Do I end up with *you*?" he asked.

"Yes, you end up with me."

His eyes lit when he smiled. "Okay," he said, "I'll dance with the guys."

AUG - 1 1994